Praise for
The Landlord of Hummingbird House
(Book One)

"Jane Harvey's *The Landlord of Hummingbird House* is cosy and warm while addressing real discomforts, regrets, and traumas."
Independent Book Review

Winner: *Eyelands International* Published Novel, 2021

Buttercups
in the
Basement

Jane Harvey

Book Two in the Hummingbird House Series

FIRST EDITION

Book Cover Design by Dreena Collins

Original Vectors (modified) by @ Lucky2084 via Deposit Photos

Published by Sherman House.

ISBN 978-1-7396126-0-3

To friendship.

Chapter One:
Betty (Now)

David was sitting on the wall outside the house, obediently, as requested. His grey t-shirt was rough and raw-edged – tatty looking to her eyes. The short sleeves were tight around his biceps. The sharp point of his black tattoo poked out from beneath the fabric on his left arm. But she reminded herself not to judge. It was a nasty habit creeping up on her, she had noticed. Unbecoming.

He seemed poised as he sat, still – hands clasped together as he stared straight ahead.

David: this elusive, kind young man. She knew some of this was a façade.

To most of his friends, he was Dai. But he indulged her and tolerated her calling him by his Christian name – just as his mother had done. She felt it suited him.

She wondered what he was thinking.

Betty spotted a young woman who she assumed to be April parking confidently nearby – her little red car squeezing neatly into the last remaining space on that side of the street. As she got out, rummaging on the seat beside her for a couple of possessions, Betty turned quietly on her heel and made her way back inside.

She hoped for happier days to come in Hummingbird House.

Perhaps this young lady was what they all needed.

*

Back in the basement, she strained to hear the sounds of David taking April on a tour of the house. She couldn't help but smile at his deep, gruff voice: monosyllabic sounds and two-word sentences croaked out of him – toad-like and brusque. Poor, dear David. He sounded fierce and unfriendly. In fact, he was simply shrivelled. Lost. Dehydrated. And sad. What on earth would this new tenant think?

She put the kettle on; the deep rumble of the water as it boiled melted into the voices and footsteps above her. She took her favourite teapot from the cupboard and considered but then dismissed the idea of cake. For some reason, there was always cake these days. She was like some stereotypical granny but without grandchildren. This would not do.

The last tenant of Number Three had been Joseph. He had stayed less than a year, though he had not left on bad terms. He and his young lady had decided to move to Ireland, where she had been raised, and Joseph had even sent her a postcard once they had settled there – it was covered in shamrocks and harps and sported a tiny leprechaun in the corner. It was the epitome of tack. She was touched, though, as this seemed to suggest that he had picked it out himself: no self-respecting Irish girl would have deigned to buy it.

She hadn't heard from him since, though this was the way that it was. To be expected.

But as far as the house went, it had not been overly happy with his presence. She had hoped – wrongly it seemed – that he might bring out the youthful side of David and Paul especially. But it wasn't to be.

Paul had been in Number Two for almost five years and had undergone quite a transformation during the first couple of those. She recalled the way he had winced, blinked, and looked away that first day while he had explained that he was looking for somewhere affordable to live alone, as he had broken up with his girlfriend. Needed a fresh start. She didn't pry, but he was still alone five years later from what she had seen. No harm in that, of course. She'd been alone for decades, herself.

When he had arrived, he was working as a chef. He would leave in the afternoon, wearing strange rubber clogs and a perpetual frown. Even on occasions when he wasn't working, he had a sort of jagged, rough look if she saw him. And on those long and frequent working days, she would hear him returning home, sometimes as late as 2 a.m.

But after about six months or so, she was surprised to bump into him coming home at 5 or 6 p.m. He was de-clogged and fresh-faced. He chuckled at the sight of her: presumably slack-jawed and agog, and he explained that he had changed his career altogether and was now working for Shelterhouse Sanctuary – a charity.

She remembered how they sat on the bench in the front yard for a short while and chatted. It was the first time he had done so, though they talked at least once a week these days. She would often see him carrying what she assumed to be a computer of some sort or clutching an over-full paper bag of vegetables or herbs. He still had the cooking bug, she gathered. Though he could only have been feeding himself.

He had no regrets, he had told her that day. Hospitality had some negative associations for him now, and he preferred feeding those who needed it rather than those who sent back their gazpacho for being 'too cold.'

Slowly but comfortably, she had gotten to know him better until he trusted her enough to confide some of their painful family history when David – his cousin –moved into the top floor with Doreen. She felt for him. For both of them. Families are rarely easy.

He was a lovely young man, as was David. And Jonty and Ben in Number One, of course. They had been with her for years now; steadfast, predictable, entertaining.

She was immensely proud of her motley crew of gentlemen in Hummingbird House. It would be interesting to see how the place shifted and stretched to accommodate the young woman she was welcoming into it.

Chapter Two:
Betty (Now)

It had been four days since April arrived, but she hadn't seen David since. She had heard him, of course. His habit of jogging down the stairs – jumping the last two or three – was unmistakable. But those fierce, frenetic forays outside had been few and far between. He seemed to be holed up on the top floor the rest of the time. She didn't think he'd even made it into Paul's flat, although there had been a time when they ate together regularly – the two cousins, usually accompanied by Doreen, David's late mother, never missing a Sunday lunch at least. She would hear the deep boom of David's teasing and laughter and the soft lullaby of Paul's dry anecdotes above her, and it was a comfort. A home.

But she hadn't heard his voice once, hadn't seen him to talk to.

Cautiously, gently, she clambered the thirty-nine stairs up to the top floor: fifteen to exit the basement, then twelve between each landing. She knew them by heart but always counted each time. As if they might miraculously change one day and morph to ten, thirteen.

She counted to take her mind off her right knee and away from the memories and dreams tangled up on each floor. She counted to regulate her breath and distract her brain from her 82-year-old bones. She had taken these steps many times before. She could have walked them with her eyes closed.

She noted again the carpet that was lifted on one of the stairs. She really must get that fixed. She spotted a cobweb hanging as a stalactite from one corner, the chipped paintwork on the newel post. The place had never been pristine, but perhaps it could do with a facelift. If a property drifts too far into disarray, it can become overwhelming to try to pull it back into order. Better to keep on top of these things.

A spring clean, at the very least.

She reached David's floor and paused. She could feel her breath, aggressive yet shallow, and the tingle of blood on her cheeks and lower lip. She waited; it would pass. It always did. She stood still a moment, one hand resting on the banister. Listening. Focusing. Then she rapped on his door and waited.

At first, there was no sound, and she wondered if he was asleep or ignoring the knock on the door. She stood still and gave him time. Unexpected guests are not always welcome. And there is nothing worse than an impatient visitor hammering away for your attention while you were trying to make yourself decent or hide the dirty cups. Or simply cursing them. She was in no rush.

She heard an internal door groan open a moment later and then the padding of feet along the corridor. He'd been in his bedroom then – or Doreen's.

He cracked the door ajar to see who it was and then opened it more fully once he saw her standing there. A good sign.

"David," she said, in an upbeat singsong, "I am so sorry to bother you. But I have a little job that I can't do alone, and I wondered if you'd be so kind as to help me again."

"Right. Will do. Yup. What's that, then?" He rubbed his hands across his face and deep into his eye sockets. He spoke quickly, hoarsely, and vacantly. She saw the shadow of his facial hair and took in the grease at the roots of the dark curls that covered and flopped about his head. He did not look good. But he remembered himself. "God, sorry. I mean, come in. Come in. I'll put the kettle on."

As it turned out, he had no tea, and the milk was off. She accepted his glass of tepid tap water, though she had no intention of drinking it. People want to feel they have been a good host to their guests. Always best to accept their offerings. She held it between her hands and noted the clouding of the glass where it had been rinsed without soap or in water that was not hot enough, perhaps.

The flat was not messy, but it had stale air to it. Closed windows; dust on the television screen; carpet not hoovered; no lights on. It was as if no one actually lived there.

"It's my new furniture. For the bedroom. It's only do-it-yourself plywood. I've ordered it, but I can't collect it. You know me, I rely on the bus these days. I am not sure they'd take too kindly to my bringing a flatpack wardrobe and two bedside cabinets aboard. Even if I could manage it." She placed the glass on the small table beside her. "Which, obviously, I can't!" She attempted a joke.

He gave a half-hearted snort in response. Then there was silence for a beat. She did not rush him.

"Didn't they offer to deliver it when you bought it?" he said. "That's not on. You know, they even take your old stuff away sometimes. For a charge, usually… anyway. Still."

"Oh, I bought it on the internet," she said. "There wasn't a delivery option. It was a 'click and collect' purchase."

He raised his left eyebrow, the clear arch rising beneath that one wayward curl that always hung over his forehead. Was she rumbled?

"The internet?" he asked, with a touch of mockery. "I didn't know you were an online shopper."

"Why yes," she said. "I'm not that decrepit, you know. I can navigate my way around a computer. Enough to buy a flat-pack wardrobe, at least. I am a silver surfer and proud." She sat back.

It was true. Once she had gotten used to the numerous steps and learnt the knack of clicking and scrolling, she rather enjoyed going online these days. She even accessed the radio that way, sometimes. Why shouldn't she?

"A silver surfer." He laughed, a sudden clear and fresh laugh. "I should have known. No doubt you're better than me. Perhaps I should get you to show me your tricks… So when and where exactly do I need to get this flatpack?"

Chapter Three:
Betty (Then)

She would not have said so aloud, but the new house filled her stomach with butterflies in a way that the wedding never had.

William had gone off with his father in his precious new Vauxhall Viva to collect more boxes and pick up a bolt for the front door. 'Daddy' had insisted, thinking they were moving to an undesirable neighbourhood. Betty chuckled inwardly at this, knowing it to be a significantly safer suburb than the one her own family had always lived in. Plus, they might have afforded a slightly nicer property if William hadn't blown some of his inheritance on that damn car (which, ironically, Daddy had encouraged). But she said nothing.

So, she was here, alone. And she finally had time. Just her and Hummingbird House.

William laughed when she said she intended to revert the house to its original title. The cracked pottery sign beside the front door said '15', but after a little digging, she had discovered more about the provenance of the house and its former name. William had been amused, saying he should have expected this sort of thing to feature in his life when he had popped the question. Daddy had frowned slightly. But she had her way and had already arranged for a new plaque to be made. He was very easy-going about such things, her new husband. Which suited her fine.

She stood outside the house for several minutes, head thrown back to take in all three floors. The small yard was edged by a privet bush, golden, somewhat unhealthy-looking leaves spiking out of shape and disguising the low wall beneath. The yard had uneven slabs, with dandelions and buttercups poking through; the vibrant yellows and greens of nature contrasting harshly with the pale blue paint of the front door – ugly, with its large, reinforced glass panels that made up most of the door, and the strange, upright letterbox.

She edged towards the door, determined to take in each detail while she had the chance. William would only comment and tease; Daddy would tell her to 'come on, come on, hurry up.' They only saw bricks and mortar. And cracks. She noted the large, grey, square slabs of the path that led to the door, the years of ingrained dirt in the older stones that made up the yard's flooring. It would be easy enough to fix up this area with a bit of elbow grease and some pots. It wouldn't be perfect, but she could make it cheery. She wasn't much of a gardener, but she could learn.

She pushed the front door ajar, wrinkling her nose at the cobweb of silver wire running through the glass panels and the lumpy, frosted surface of the glass. The wood was crumbling in the frame, poking through the paint like strands of tobacco as it met the panels. No doubt, this had not helped Daddy's opinion of the neighbourhood. But she doubted this security was needed; plus, she already had a new door in mind. The previous owners had either been paranoid or held many more valuables than they did.

She could picture it – an entrance more in keeping with the property. It was Georgian. Needed something classic. She would do her research and start the slow – almost overwhelming – journey to bring it back to its former glory.

The corridor was laid with a beige, speckled linoleum that had seen better days. Orange and brown dots covered the surface and gave an oddly disorientating effect when paired with pale green wallpaper that filled the stairwell – the geometric design replicated dozens of times before her. It must have been ten years old, at least. Surely, she could persuade William to replace it.

She entered the front room, which she had already decided would be the sitting room (or drawing-room, as William would say). The vast window was buried under layers of stained nets. She had an urge to yank them down but had nothing to put up in their place. Instead, she burrowed within them until her head poked through, and she could look outside again.

Betty wondered what Mum, Dorothy, would make of this vast, tatty house that they had purchased. And it was unnecessarily large: there was no denying it. She couldn't bear the thought of allowing Mum to visit until at least this room was presentable – with her strange, penniless snobbery at anything poorly maintained. Faded, worn, old, these things didn't matter to Mum as long as everything was clean, pressed, and polished. She was ruthlessly judgemental about poorly swept yards and dirty windows. She pictured her now;

nose wrinkled upwards like an unfriendly cat. She would be blatantly disgusted. Looking to find fault in a home that she, herself, could never afford.

"And I bet that will set you back a pretty penny," she muttered when Betty told her about the house. She had ignored the comment and continued to describe it excitedly. Mum listened silently, never once looking up from the ironing board, moving her pressing cloth in an orderly pattern around her brother's shirt as Betty spoke. She stood in the centre of her sitting room, with a rag rug in front of the gas fire to disguise where the colour was faded in the carpet, a blanket thrown over the worn arm of her brother's chair. Yet you would be hard pushed to find a solitary speck of dust.

Betty attempted to draw her in, laughing, animated, as she described how the back door had been missing from the mid-point down. "The garden was starting to advance and reclaim it," she said. "There was so much mud and grit covering the old doormat that there was even a weed growing out of it." She laughed, but Mum remained stony-faced. Tutted.

"Aren't you going to tell me then? Or don't you talk about money now that you're Miss La-di-dah?"

"Tell you what?"

"You know full well. The cost, Miss Bigwig."

"I… £2,900," she said.

Mum stopped.

"What? Never." She put the cloth down, blinking furiously. "You could have bought one of those new semi-detached ones with a front garden up by Chessington Grove for that price. Jeanie's boy is looking to get one with a driveway. A driveway.

12

And what have you got? No front garden and buttercups in the basement. What were you thinking?"

"I was thinking of improving it. Making it somewhere special."

"You were, were you? How exactly are you going to do that? Your William's not really handy with a toolbox now, is he? And it's not like you've got some vast mound of pounds and shillings under your mattress."

"Maybe not, but he can learn… and… and so could I." She regretted saying it the moment the words came out of her mouth. Her mum's face said it all.

"Over my dead body," Mum said. "You're already 27. You need to settle down to raise a family, not swanning around in your *cigarette pants*," she gave a withering glance at her trousers, "carrying a hammer and nails."

"It's 1967, Mum. I'm not talking about becoming a bloody roofer. I can learn how to put up a picture frame if I want to."

"Your father would…" she started but trailed off. "And mind your bloody language."

Betty looked up at her mother and met her eyes for the first time, shocked to note that they were glistening wet. She was a strange creature, this woman. Who knew what she honestly thought? Who could fathom what actually worried her? The sight of her, someone so rarely emotional, softened Betty. She stood and moved towards her mum, placing one hand on hers.

"It'll be fine, Mum. You'll get your grandchildren, I promise. And you can come around for a cup of tea soon. You'll see. It's not as bad as you think."

Her mum blinked and looked away and then picked the cloth up again as if to resume her work – but it stayed there a moment, hanging limp in her fingers like a white flag.

Chapter Four:
Betty (Then)

Three and a bit weeks later, Betty was supervising the installation of a new front door, listening intently as the carpenter told her about the colour television that his son had just purchased. He'd been around to the neighbours to watch Wimbledon and came home 'full of it,' he had said.

"He had a windfall when the mother-in-law passed on at the start of the year. A tidy sum – hundreds it was. More than I could have dreamt of at his age. And he already had a bit of cash stashed away, which he'd earmarked for a ring for his girl. That went out the window. She's none too happy, I can tell you. And then he goes and wins at the bookies – not much mind. Just enough to tip him over. Lucky sod. And the next thing you know, he's gone and done it."

The man paused and shook his head, but she could sense his admiration. He couldn't have been more than fifty, she estimated, but he was clearly in awe of his own son.

"Goodness," Betty said. She had never met someone with a colour television. Even William's wealthiest relations didn't have one.

"Not that his mother is too happy. She didn't expect him to blow it all, like that." He sucked the air through his teeth.

"Have you seen it?" Betty asked. "What's it like?"

"Oh yes," he said, as he continued to screw away, "A great huge ruddy thing it is. The screen, too. A big bright picture. Gives me a blooming headache. But it's quite something. It's quite something."

Betty glanced into their sitting room, devoid of a television altogether. They would never have bought a colour one of course, but many of her friends had black and white sets. It was one of the few things that William was insistent upon. He hated them; he wanted to spend evenings doing what he termed 'more erudite things.' Reading, walking, even singing – in the house, of course. They did not go out often. Usually, she didn't mind the lack of television. But listening to this story of the new colour screen and how the neighbours all camped around it, she felt a moment of jealousy that she was missing out, perhaps. It was the company that she craved, more than the programmes.

Betty turned away. "I'd better stop distracting you," she said.

He was still shaking his head, softly smiling, as she stepped away.

He was an unusual man, her William. She had always known this, of course. It was part of what attracted her to him in the first place. He had bright, intense passions for some things – his car, certain foods, strange, obscure historical facts. But the ideas and items that enamoured him were few and far between. Most things he thought of as unnecessary and vaguely amusing – especially modern gadgets and quirks.

And she had discovered that he was more than happy to allow her to make the decisions, gleefully making a show of putting his pay packet into the same drawer each week, having told her from day one that he couldn't be bothered 'fannying about with some sort of housekeeping allowance.' He expected her to help herself as needed without question. And to take care of all the bills.

She obliged, enjoying the responsibility, and finding that she was good at seeking out a bargain or hammering down the price on a deal. Things William was useless at, having never had a need. They made a great team. She didn't mention this arrangement to her mother, of course.

And considering he had come from such a comfortable home, he did not seem to bat an eyelid at the more squalid aspects of their new house. Each day, she encountered more issues, more damp, more damage, and he would laugh and almost skip with delight when she relayed her stories as he arrived home from the office.

"A mouse! How fascinating!" he'd say, pulling her towards him for a kiss.

"You won't be calling it fascinating when we both get the bubonic plague," she'd counter, laughing as he looked around dramatically with mock horror and pretended to hear something.

They'd eat dinner together, at their small table, and she would spend the evening scraping the paint from cupboards or skirting boards, carrying her transistor radio from room to room, while he sat in the one good chair, sketching, or reading his paper.

Sometimes, she would pause, and sit back on her haunches, only to notice him watching her, smiling contentedly. And she would wink and smile back.

He was an affectionate man. Demonstrative. He would scoop her up in his arms and twirl her, give her big, hard kisses on her cheek, her forehead, her neck, even. But his affection was playful and effusive, rather than sensual and intense. Sometimes, she tried to encourage his more passionate side, and build on those moments of affection in the hope of something more.

They had been married for four months now, and at first, she had assumed that the lack of passion in the bedroom was because they were living with his parents. But now, there was no excuse. They'd been in Hummingbird House for several weeks and hadn't yet made love once since they arrived. It was confusing, even hurtful, receiving hugs, kisses, laughter, and then lying next to him in bed, hearing his breath deepen and shift into a soft purr as he fell asleep without touching her. And she felt a rising fear with each week as she edged towards her twenty-eighth birthday, still childless. She knew that she was going to have to broach the subject out loud at some stage, but she had no idea how.

Chapter Five:
Betty (Now)

David was sitting in her flat, next to Oxo, the cat from Number One, who had taken up his usual spot on the green velvet cushion.

"I would offer to put it together for you," he said. "But I am useless. Really awful." The boxes of flat-pack furniture lay next to his feet on the floor.

Betty laughed and assured him she wouldn't be asking, after what had happened on the occasion that he had tried to fix a bolt to her flat door. She saw his face morph from a shocked smile to a wince at the memory and wondered if she had touched a nerve. It had been quite a disaster, with David making three holes in the doorframe before admitting defeat. She had ended up doing it herself, though she hadn't told anyone. At first, her gnarled fingers objected to the twisting and force, but in the end, she succeeded. The arthritis that plagued the base of her thumb hurt for over a week afterwards. But it was worth it.

She had managed to get him out of the house, to collect the flatpack, and he had even showered before he went. Now he was sitting with her in the flat. This was progress. Each step. Small. She was satisfied. He had even agreed to cake. Next, she needed him to interact with people his own age.

It is a dreadful thing, grief. Doreen had passed away months ago now, and yet this young man carried the pain about him like a raw, fresh wound. He was lacerated by his mother's death. That would be the guilt, layered and interwoven with the loss. She knew what that felt like, that peculiar mixture of blame and pain, though she was thankful she had never experienced it to the extent young David clearly had – almost, but not quite. And yet she didn't think David was to blame. Not at all. He had done a hundred times more than most other sons would have done.

But it is hard, so hard, to save someone intent on remaining lost. And one thing was certain, David had tried his hardest to help his mother. And he loved her. That was all that really mattered.

Earlier that day, as she was arriving home from the hairdressers, she had passed April, who said she was leaving to meet her sister. They had chatted, then, albeit briefly, but it occurred to Betty that she'd be returning home any time now – at least, judging by the plans she had shared. A car trip to her sister's, who was making her lunch in exchange for a lift back to Hummingbird House to see April's handiwork in the flat. She was chipping away at improving it, she had told her. And she seemed proud of her work. Betty knew that feeling.

She placed the two china mugs on the tray, along with the fruit cake she had made yesterday, and started to make her way towards the stairs, wordlessly. If she was lucky, not only would she extend David's stay out of his flat, and get him up and out, but they might even get to chat with the new tenant. Either way, there was no harm in getting this young man some more fresh air. She heard him shuffle and clear his throat. But he was too polite to comment, or decline.

She smiled as she sensed him make his way behind her and take the tray, to help her. Oxo came with them.

*

"Have you ever thought of having a pet, David?" Betty asked him, as he leant forward to touch the cat's sleek back. He was slinking his way between their legs, pushing against their trousers and purring. David opened his mouth to speak when the cat suddenly leapt away with a slight hiss, for no apparent reason. They both laughed.

"Because I have quite the way with animals?" he asked.

She smiled. "They can be great company. I never understand these landlords that won't allow them. The chances of them making permanent damage to a property are minuscule. And they make a house a home. Plus, this way, I get to live vicariously and get all the benefits of homing a cat without any of the responsibilities."

"Or bills," David said, leaning, rubbing his fingers together and trying to tempt Oxo back.

"That's rather what I meant," she said. "I am his, but he is not mine."

"*I am his, but he is not mine,*" David repeated and cocked his head. "Yeah… No. I haven't ever had a cat or a dog. Not since I was a kid. I don't know why, really. Maybe I should." He turned back to her.

21

"You wouldn't mind? Another cat in the house, I mean?"

"*I* certainly wouldn't. Oxo, here, is the one who might have a problem with it." She smiled. "No… I am joking. I'm sure it would be fine. He'd get used to it eventually. You know, I did once have two cats of my own. But that was a long time ago now."

"Maybe I will." He slapped his thighs. "Maybe I will get a cat. Some old raggedy, poorly thing which needs somewhere comfy to spend their last few years. I'll just… get back on my… get back to work first. And then maybe I will. Yeah."

"You have plenty of space," she said. He didn't answer, and they both drank from their mugs in silence, until David yawned and stood after a moment, moving around the small yard awkwardly as if stretching his legs. She knew he wanted to leave.

"Now, David, I know what I was going to tell you. I saw that lovely girl who used to visit you, the other day. I couldn't for the life of me remember her name. The one with short black hair. She used to go out running with you. She said hello to me: 'Betty! Oo!' from the other side of the street," she mimicked. "And I felt rather rude as I couldn't recall her name for love nor money."

"Oh! You mean Ali. Alison," he said, with a slight grin.

"Alison! Of course. How rude of me."

"Not really," he said. "It was yonks ago now – eighteen months at least – and I wasn't… didn't spend time with her for long. Only a couple of weeks."

Betty knew it had been substantially longer than that but didn't like to push the issue. Alison had even joined them at one of their end-of-summer barbecues. She could recall her, playfighting with him, sitting on his lap, gazing at him. She clearly adored him. He had been nice enough towards her, but she had suspected at the time that he didn't feel the same. This proved to be true when Alison stopped coming around altogether shortly afterwards.

"You aren't friends anymore, then?" she asked, looking down into her mug. She wasn't sure the words to use.

"*Friends*, yes. I guess so. More than that... no. Never really were. Or not exactly. Not on my side, anyway. She was a lovely girl, but it's hard to explain. I didn't... I don't... It's not often I get those kinds of feelings – no, not feelings. I don't know. Sorry. Oversharing. Ha!" He gave a fake little awkward laugh. "Somehow, I've never been too bothered about having a girl. I think that's what I mean. I liked her and all that. But it didn't seem fair when she wanted something else. She is really lovely..." He trailed off. "Sorry, that probably doesn't make any sense."

"On the contrary," she answered, quietly. "I think I know exactly what you mean."

"Having a party without us? How dare you!" Jonty called out of the window, making her jump. He and Ben were leaning out, tickled at the sight of Betty and David together on a sunny afternoon.

Betty chuckled. "You're welcome to join us. There's more fruit cake."

David looked to the ground, seemingly to keep an eye on his plate, which was balanced precariously on the edge of a planter.

Jonty and Ben went away briefly, and she assumed they would come outside to join them, but it seemed they liked the comfort of the indoors too much to want to share a garden bench. They came back a few moments later, soft drinks in hand, and the wireless turned up. They leant against the window and pulled the sheer curtains apart, giving a brief glimpse of their tidy but unarguably cluttered apartment. A piano, many plants, too much furniture. It was too small for them, in truth. Perhaps they would move on, at some stage, too. She didn't enjoy the thought.

"Here comes trouble!" called Ben, as April and another woman – unmistakeably the sister she had mentioned – approached. Their walk was synchronised. Between them trotted a small white dog.

April was quick to join in, smiling broadly at Ben. "Speak for yourself," she said before turning to Dai. "Don't worry; it's not my dog."

Betty was amused to note that April still seemed to be under the misapprehension that David was the landlord. She had no intention of dissuading her.

He stared at her for a moment and shrugged. Betty marvelled at how quickly he had pulled away again. He was a flame, extinguished. Just when she had seen a flash – a spark of his old self, and his trust – he was gone again. Armoured and retreated.

Everyone else chattered away comfortably as April's sister's little white dog sniffed about the yard. Oxo was nowhere to be seen, Betty noted.

24

These were the afternoons she loved. This was the company she craved. She adored these wonderful young people, with their openness, and their easy ways. Then after a short while, Paul joined them, too. She saw his surprise at David being outside among them and gave her a furtive thumbs up when he wasn't looking – with a swift nod in his direction.

But then, a few moments later, David was gone again; slipped back upstairs and away inside his grief.

Chapter Six:
Betty (Then)

The summer was a hot one. Betty battled against the dry air, her skin dewy and salted by the end of the day. William laughed at her, her hair tied back in an old scarf, and trousers smudged with dust and paint by the end of each day. Her mum would have been mortified, which was why she still hadn't invited her around to visit, much to her suspicion and disapproval.

But Betty was determined to complete as many of the smaller jobs as possible by herself and had discovered that she was quite good at it, contrary to her mum's disparaging comments. If that involved getting dirty and never quite finding the right time to wear her new orange mini-skirt, so be it.

Alone by day, she had taken to kicking off her shoes, humming along to the songs on her transistor. Without her mother – or William – there to censor her taste, she was fully exposed to the news and music of the day for the first time. Ever. Race riots in the United States. *Mary Quant* in London. Remarkable new roadways being built, with three lanes and few junctions. She listened in for eight, sometimes ten hours a day. It was invigorating.

With great speed and efficiency, by the middle of July she had transformed the basement into a small apartment. It was basic, and probably needed some more substantial work in the long term, but it was certainly liveable.

When they had moved in, it was a somewhat neglected space that looked as if it might have been used as a place for parents or an older sibling to stay. There was a rudimentary but not functioning kitchen, and an old single bed with a rusted metal frame, on cracked lino flooring. William had joked that they could house her mum there, but Betty didn't even deign to reply to that.

She had arranged for it to be cleared, and the back door replaced, and then spent the next days cleaning, scrubbing, and painting the walls. New flooring was laid – bright yellow carpet against the shiny white paintwork. All that was left to install was a hob and a refrigerator. She had been careful to choose one with a new frost-free icebox, knowing what a benefit this was to the cook of the house. A little pricier, but William was none the wiser. This was the benefit of being the purse-holder.

So now they were almost ready to make this into a rental property. They would have a small income and could start to save to improve the rest of the house. And they would have company.

Just in time for her twenty-eighth birthday.

*

The advert in the corner shop window had led to several knocks on the door. They weren't yet on the telephone, though they did have William's mother's old black cast-off sitting patiently in the hallway, waiting to be connected. She secretly aspired to install a bright yellow or red handset once they had finally replaced the hideous wallpaper, but that was likely to be some time yet.

She had already been visited by a young man, who had unsettled her by wanting to see the place there and then. She had obliged but afterwards had vouched to stand her ground with any future visitors and arrange for them to come back at a time that suited her, rather than them. She stood while he examined the place in great detail, feeling uncomfortable in her scruffy outfit with unbrushed hair. He had fired off a series of questions and told her he'd be back the next day either way. She'd not heard from him again and was relieved.

Then there was an older couple who had clearly been unimpressed by the yellow carpet and the smoked-glass lamp she had placed on a dresser. She had thought it striking and right on trend and was proud of her bargain purchase.

"That's *unusual*," the gentleman had muttered through pursed lips. Unusually terrible, was the implication.

At the end of the viewing, she was irritated enough to tell him that as she had lots of interest in the place she was considering charging more. Would they still be interested? They had left quickly after that. William had been delighted when she told him about it.

Today she was waiting for a young couple. William vaguely knew the young man – a friend of a friend – and she felt optimistic as it seemed they were broadly the same age. And the connection, tenuous as it was, gave her hope that they might be of a similar mind. Surely his friend would not recommend somebody dreadful.

He worked as an engineer, designing kitchen appliances, William said. She was an artist, and he wasn't sure what she did, but she had another job of some sort too, he gathered. So, they had a good enough income and weren't layabouts (as he put it).

An artist and an engineer. She marvelled at this, realising with a jolt how much she craved some company – spending most days, as she did, in the home alone. And she felt somewhat plain and boring in comparison. She had tied her hair back, put on some eye makeup (a rarity for her), and even wore her new orange mini-skirt in honour of their visit.

Punctually, at 4 o'clock, there was a rap at the front door. She paused, thinking for some reason that she would seem more important and respectable if she forced them to wait, and then after the briefest of moments, she made her way to the hallway. Through the mottled grey glass, she could make out the shape of three people.

"Welcome," she said as she opened the door. Her voice sounded high and false, but the woman on the other side broke into a broad smile.

"Thank the Lord," she said. "I was worried you'd be some sort of square."

*

She was Sandra. "This is Robert," she said, pointing to the shorter of the two gentlemen who shuffled close behind her as they made their way downstairs. "You can call him anything you like, except Bob."

"Right-o," Betty said, unsure how to respond. Robert nodded at her and winked but didn't speak.

The other gentleman had remained silent so far, and no one mentioned him. He was impeccably dressed, with a starched shirt and matching striped neck scarf tied jauntily – unlike Robert, who wore straight-legged dark green trousers, socks showing, and a long, brown leather jacket, even though it was July. She noted the hem was loose on one leg– instantly annoyed to find a glimmer of her mother surfacing once more.

"You have your own entrance," Betty said, "but I thought we'd go in this way for the ease of directions. The flat is on the basic side, but all newly decorated and surprisingly light."

They reached the bottom of the stairs, and Sandra stood still, beaming, as she looked around. Betty enjoyed the moment, glad that her work and taste were appreciated; surprised to find a small pang of regret that the space would no longer be hers, alone, in the near future.

"This is great," she said. She reached out and tapped Betty's forearm, absently, as she took in the room.

Robert whistled softly. "Yeah, far out."

"Well, this carpet is very cheery." The third man spoke, all of a sudden. His voice was soft and singsong. His enunciation was clear and clipped. Betty looked over at him and smiled.

"I chose it. I like it, too."

"Good taste, darling," he said. "May I?" He nodded towards the closed door of the bedroom.

"Of course." She felt herself blush.

"Make yourself at home, brother dear," Sandra said.

"I… there is only one bedroom, though. I'm not sure what you…" She trailed off.

"Don't worry. He's just doing his protective brother thing," Sandra answered. "We have no intention of letting him move in with us. This is going to be a home for two."

"I see. Do you have a home already, or are you newlyweds?"

"Ah, no. Neither. It seems brother dear isn't doing too well at protecting his little sis. Not that he's the epitome of virtue himself. We'll be living *in sin*." Sandra was idly wandering around the kitchen area, opening drawers, and looking at plug sockets.

"I… I see. Right-o," Betty said.

*

William was grinning and nodding as she spoke.

"They are rather glamorous in a way. He did tell me what he does for a living in more detail, but I had no idea and smiled and nodded. Something about design and time-saving in the kitchen. Her brother was there, and he was quite sharp and dapper. A bit more traditional, I suppose, in a way, but very discerning. A proper grown-up. And I asked her about her artwork. Apparently, they're these huge abstract pictures of people. 'Not for the faint-hearted,' she told me. Nudy bits and things," she giggled. She was laying the table as she spoke, straightening the cruet set and putting out some sliced bread.

31

"And she manages to make money that way? She must be good, I suppose," he said.

"Yes, I think so, but she does have some other job, as you said. I think it's in a café or something. 'Serving the bourgeoisie,' she described it as."

He raised his eyebrows.

"She was clearly joking, dear," Betty said. "It seems extremely unlikely that we're going to be renting out to a bunch of radical Communists."

"I should think the word 'radical' is redundant in that sentence," he muttered. "So, you've given it to them, then? They are our new tenants?"

"No, but I did like them. Thought I'd best ask what you thought, though. They were rather more *trendy* than us." She looked at him, trying to gauge his response.

"My dear old married woman. We aren't in the grave yet. And you know I trust your judgement. No need to check in with me." He slipped off his shoes and went to loosen his tie.

Betty kissed him and led him by the hand to sit down at the dinner table. She pictured Robert, with his kind eyes and soft waves drifting over his collar; Sandra grinning with her thick bob and fringe, clutching her small, bright green purse.

"I think it's going to be fun," Betty said.

Chapter Seven:
Betty (Now)

Betty stayed stock still when she heard the now-familiar rattle of April's knock on the door of the basement flat. She wasn't backwards in coming forwards, this new tenant. It was amusing. Usually, Betty would oblige and be glad of the company, but there were half a dozen reasons she simply couldn't face seeing the poor girl today – not least because she was ashamed to find herself still in her dressing gown although it was approaching lunchtime.

It seemed likely that April was looking for company while her boiler was being repaired – as Betty knew it was – which, of course, could take some time. She had a feeling April might launch into some sort of tirade about maintenance, and that would mean dissuading her of her belief that David was the landlord. And she had been enjoying watching that story, that tango, unfold, built on mistaken identities and assumptions. Mischievous? Yes. But she had little in the form of entertainment these days. Besides, it might force the two of them to interact, which couldn't be a bad thing. They both seemed lonely, in their own ways. It wasn't simply for her benefit. She smiled.

She heard April try Jonty and Ben, but Betty also knew they were away visiting Jonty's mother for a couple of days. She had the spare sack of cat food to prove it. So then she craned her neck to listen as April approached Paul's door, as she had suspected she would. Paul was in and would not appreciate the interruption but would – of course – be too polite to turn her away. Betty stifled a small laugh as she caught the sound of their muffled voices above her, continuing into his flat after a few moments, as he welcomed her in.

She was a bulldozer, that young woman. Though benign.

Betty decided on one more pot of tea before she would wash and dress. It was unusual for her to deviate from her routine and to be unpresentable at this time, but even her herbal tea and nip of whisky had not helped her to sleep the previous night, so she was taking things slowly today. Plus, she had woken before six. Such was the way things were these days, it seemed.

She felt the dull ache of arthritis in the bones on the back of her hand and at the base of her thumb as she lifted the kettle to pour boiling water into the pot. She would not go back to that patronising doctor, who told her it was to be expected 'at her age' but offered no actual advice. Whether the cause was age-related or not, she would have preferred a proper diagnosis and suggestions for treatment. He didn't even examine her, let alone send her for x-rays or blood tests.

"Not much I can say for the hands, Mrs Williams. But for your feet, you could treat yourself to some comfy shoes," he had said, louder and more slowly than necessary. He looked down to her feet, where she wore low-heeled red, leather court shoes.

"Are there any exercises I could do?" she asked.

"*Ex*-ercises, Mrs Williams?" he had repeated, staring quizzically at the prescription for painkillers that he had in his hand, midway to passing it over to her. She wondered why he felt the need to say her name so often. Was it designed to jog her memory or his?

"I appreciate that – assuming it is arthritis – it is wear and tear, but I wondered if there was anything pro-active I could do to prevent further decline. Or something dietary, perhaps? Supplements?"

He gave a low chuckle and shook his head. "You can't turn back the clock, Mrs Williams. Supplements can't cure arthritis." As if, by any stretch of the imagination, she would have thought that they could.

If only.

She put the teapot and her favourite cup on a tray and retrieved the milk pot from the fridge. She might have to consider a new fridge soon, she realised, as the under-the-counter design of this one, with its low shelves and creaky door, was becoming increasingly awkward to bend down to, especially for anything that made its way to the back. That was a worry for another day.

She carried the tray into the living area, avoiding the velvet cushion that Oxo the cat frequented. Instead, she sat at the other end, where her occasional table was within reach, as was the radio. She switched to Radio 2.

Her mind drifted to dear Ben and Jonty, diligently visiting Jonty's elderly mother again. He would return with a packet of fudge or biscuits to thank her feeding the cat, and show her miniature photographs on his mobile phone, no doubt. She always looked forward to their return after these trips. The pair of them burst in with enthusiasm and joy. She loved to hear the stories of his mother and her outrageous antics, tearing up the local village and upsetting all the neighbours, although she was in her late 70s herself.

"Good for her!" Betty would pronounce. "I'm glad someone is misbehaving in their twilight years."

And Jonty would be delighted at her validation and say how much he hoped they'd get to meet up one day. Secretly, she rather hoped so, too.

She strained the tea into her cup and took in the robust and smoked smell of the Lapsang Souchong. The steam rose up, moistening the back of her hand, almost scalding her thin skin.

One day she'd do something outrageous, too, she thought to herself. One day, soon.

Chapter Eight
Betty (Now)

A couple of days later, Betty bumped into April as she was taking some rubbish downstairs, as Betty had decided to catch the afternoon sun, out the front of Hummingbird House. As Betty greeted April, her voice croaked, and she realised that it was the first time she had spoken aloud that day. This was not good. Not for the first time, she considered whether it was time to begin attending some form of social club or centre for people 'her age'. She preferred the company of younger people, in the main, but they were all so busy and preoccupied, it often left her at a loose end. Besides, frankly, perhaps they also preferred the company of youngsters. Maybe they didn't want to spend time with *her*. The thought of being an imposition – worse still, *tolerated* – made her shudder.

She encouraged the young lady to talk: easy, as she seemed one to need little excuse to chatter. A few pointed questions and she was away. April made the mistake of relaying how she was putting new curtains up herself, and how she was thinking of putting up coat hooks by the door. Betty saw her opportunity; it didn't take much persuasion for her to agree to go to Betty's flat to put her new bedside cabinets together.

They were downstairs within fifteen minutes.

April made short work of it. Betty admired the confidence with which she tackled the flatpack. She folded out the instructions and scanned them, then arranged all the pieces in an orderly fashion before her, but afterwards rarely seemed to glance at the sheet at all. Was this talent, youth, confidence, luck, or skill? Betty pottered about her; fluffing cushions, wiping the surfaces in the kitchen. The first cabinet was finished in around twenty minutes. She thought back to the times when she had first moved into Hummingbird House: hazy memories of sanding skirting boards and changing cupboard handles mingled together.

"Have a cup of tea before you start that second lot," Betty said. There was a tap on the flat door. "I wonder who that could be?" She was pleased to hear the knock, wondering if either Paul or David would be on the other side of the door. She would be glad to see either of them, for differing reasons.

It was David. He looked tired, worn, and had visibly lost more weight. She stopped herself from commenting on it. "We're having tea. Do come in, David," Betty said. She hoped he would. He clearly needed to.

"Won't stop," he replied, voice gruffer than usual. He seemed to be addressing Betty but he was looking down at April, clearly bothered to find her there.

Betty noted that as April looked up, he looked away. What had become of this young man? Where was his easy company, his good humour?

"Come now. You're sure you don't want tea, my David? It's no trouble, as April is due a break." She tried to say it in a way that gave him little choice, polite as he was. Yet still, he resisted.

"No, thanks. Just wanted to say I'll be using, going out... you know, out there... tonight. If you don't mind." He gestured towards the rear of the property, somehow unable to articulate the fact that he was going to the shed to sort his mother's possessions. Betty felt a twinge. How far away he had drifted.

She smiled. "You really don't need to ask me," she reminded him. She lifted one hand up and touched his arm to reiterate it. How many times had they had this verbal dalliance? Yet he kept his eyes to the ground, apologetic, and humble, and she watched as he rushed to leave. He turned quickly on his heel and moved to the stairs, calling goodbye absent-mindedly over his shoulder. This one short interaction seemed to be all he could cope with.

She wondered if she might pop out to see him later. Bring him tea. Encourage him to eat.

"Bye, David," April teased, as he left. Betty felt her hackles rise. Mockery seemed cruel. But of course, this young woman didn't know the full importance of what she said. *David*. So Betty watched in silence as he flinched, shoulders rising in a reflex at the name that so few people seemed to use for him. Just Betty, and his late mother.

Chapter Nine:
Betty (Then)

Sandra and Robert were moving in – a raggle-taggle crew of young people and relatives shifting cardboard boxes and heavy suitcases in via the back door, while others pulled up to the front in unhelpfully small Minis and rusted Ford Cortinas. They seemed to have a large, eclectic, chirpy group of friends, ranging from young women with teased hair and immaculate nails to older men who rolled up the sleeves on their striped cotton shirts. Betty propped the sitting room door open and enjoyed the noise of people in the house, for once.

She had made herself tea and was humming along to The Spencer Davis group on her transistor when Sandra appeared at her door. Betty was delighted to see her, having felt that she was missing out, somehow. Odd given the awkwardness and labour of the tasks, but true. She'd even been tempted to offer to help, but then wondered if that would be an odd move for a landlady.

"Hello," Sandra said. "Sorry to bother you."

"Not at all! How can I help?" She gestured for her to come in, but Sandra stayed put with a quick flick of her hair. She leant into the room, hands on the door frame, her small bird-like arms holding her upper body weight. She swung back and forth quickly. Betty wondered if she might fall.

"I wondered if we could get the key to the front door? We only have the back door key at the moment and… this could take a while. Not sure about keeping the front door propped open when the evening starts drawing in."

Betty felt a pang of disappointment that it was something so mundane, though unsure of what exactly she had been hoping for. She was truly silly, sometimes.

"Yes, that makes sense but I'm afraid it's my husband who has the front door keys for you. He went to get them cut today – or at least, I hope he did. We've been a bit slow off the blocks with that, I'm afraid. He'll be back around a quarter to six, though. It'll still be light then."

"Ah, right. As long as you don't mind. Didn't want to be taking liberties."

Betty smiled. "I'm not overly concerned. And neither will William be."

"William?"

"Yes. My husband." She still wasn't used to that word. It felt awkward in her mouth.

"But… isn't your surname Williams? Betty Williams?" Sandra asked, confused.

"I – yes it is."

"William… Williams? Wow!" Sandra clapped her hands together, gleefully.

"Yes, sort of. William is his middle name. It's a kind of family tradition. It's his father's name, too. But he goes by Bill. William – my William that is – his actual name is Frank. But don't tell him I told you." She didn't know why she asked her not to tell; for some reason, she hoped that Sandra might feel

41

they shared a confidence. But in truth, William couldn't care a fig.

"William Williams. Bill Williams. Willy Williams. Well, I never." Sandra shook her head gently, a faint smile on her lips.

"It's scorching, isn't it? I can't say I've noticed the benefit yet, but keeping the doors open seems like a good plan at the moment." Betty was keen to move off the subject.

"Absolutely. I can't believe the heat. I've been going to bed starkers for weeks and I still can't sleep."

Betty felt a red flush rise up on her neck.

"Can I get you some lemonade?" she asked.

"I…" Sandra looked over her shoulder into the corridor behind her, where two young men were struggling with a rattan peacock chair. She pulled a sheepish face and ducked fully into the room.

"Why not?" she said. "I think I've earnt a quick break."

She followed Betty towards the back of the ground floor, where a small door took them into the kitchen-diner.

"Hey," Sandra said. "This place is a bit of a maze, isn't it? It feels different to downstairs, somehow."

"Yes, it's the layout. But it's too big really." She opened a cupboard and retrieved two tall glasses. "I mean… sorry, that sounds awfully 'Lady of the Manor.' I just mean it wasn't the most sensible purchase. More rooms than we need or can afford to renovate right now. But I fell in love with it when I saw it. It has so much potential."

"Yeah, I can see why. Who'd want one of those ghastly new bungalows popping up everywhere?

I'm all for mod-cons and all that, but I also like things with a bit of soul, you know what I mean? A bit of heart and history."

The two women held a glass each and sipped. Up close, Betty could see a mist of perspiration on Sandra's brow, mingling with her chalky makeup.

"I love your dress," Betty said, for want of something to say. Though it was true. It was a short, angular, shift dress with a black and white geometric pattern.

"Regretting the choice now," Sandra said. "Keep flashing me knickers every time I pick a box up."

Betty gave a nervous giggle and looked away, taking another sip.

"I was wondering how old you are, Betty? If that's not a cheeky thing to ask. But then, I've always been a nosey bugger… I'm twenty-six if that helps."

"Oh, OK. I'm twenty-seven."

Sandra opened her eyes wide and looked at her over the top of her glass. "Really? Well, I never," she said, again.

Betty laughed, "What does that mean? Did you think I was older?"

"To be honest, I had no bloody clue. Sometimes I thought you were all grown-up and lady-like, so you must be older, but other times I've had the feeling you were younger." She finished her drink. "Like right now, for example." She said it with a smile, but Betty blushed, nonetheless.

Betty coughed on the remains of her lemonade. "I…" she trailed off, noises and coughing and laughter meshing into one.

"God, I'm sorry. I'm teasing. Please don't evict me," Sandra said, grabbing Betty's arm. "It's meant to be a joke. You'll get used to me, honest."

*

A little before six o'clock, William arrived home. By then, Betty was in the small bedroom of the basement flat, feeding curtain hooks through some 'nets' and chatting to Sandra's brother, who turned out to be called Nigel. He was mocking the quality of the fabric, aghast that Sandra had apparently bought them in Woolworths.

"I mean, not only are they one year out of style but they aren't even bloody Nylon," he said, deliberately raising his voice for Sandra to hear in the next room, though she was steadfastly ignoring him. "*Bargain bin*," he whispered, pointedly, and pretended to shudder.

Betty was laughing as William came in, bemused. No one had challenged him or even acknowledged his presence. "So, which of these many workers are my new tenants?" he asked Betty, kissing her on the cheek.

"Not this one, but he's still worth an introduction as he's Sandra's brother. I told you about him." She gestured over to Nigel.

"Now then," Nigel said, "I was optimistic at the start of that sentence, darling, when you said I was worthy of note – but then I gather that is only due to association with my younger sibling. Crushed. Crushed, I tell you." He clasped his hands to his chest briefly, and then confidently placed one out towards William for shaking.

44

"Nigel. And you must be… William, wasn't it?" He glanced to Betty for confirmation. "Give me some skin, old fella. Delighted to meet you."

The two men stood and chatted comfortably for a short while, about the house, and their respective jobs. They worked in a similar part of town and sometimes frequented the same places – not that William was much of a one for after-work drinks and the like. Betty had almost finished sorting the net curtains, smiling at their familiarity with each other, when Sandra came in.

"There you are," Betty said. "William, sorry to drag you away, but this is Sandra. One of the actual tenants." She pulled a face at Nigel, to tease him.

"William. I am so sorry about all this fuss and noise. You must think we are a terrible pain," Sandra said, stepping towards him. She had to avoid a small mound of boxes stacked precariously on the floor, to move towards him.

"Not at all. Needs must," he replied.

"Is Robert about?" Betty asked. "May as well get all the introductions done at once."

"He's… he's off somewhere out back, I think. Tied up." She looked to the floor. "How are those curtains coming along? I heard the insults flying from brother dear. I'm not paying more, when you can only see the top few inches from the outside, seeing as we are cave-dwellers now." She nudged him, playfully, and he wrinkled his nose in the direction of the net curtains, again.

"Done," Betty said, holding them out towards her, proudly.

"Don't worry, we'll soon brighten the place up." Sandra took the curtains from Betty, carefully.

"Yes," Nigel said, chuckling, "It will be all bosoms and bottoms on the walls in no time, just you see."

*

Later that evening, the last of the helpers seemed to have gone and all the doors of the house were finally closed. Betty and William sat in easy silence in their sitting room, him cradling a beer and her with a small glass of Mateus Rosé. He was in his chair, and she sat at his feet on the floor. She could see small tufts of dust beneath the sofa, and noted that the bottom drawer of the sideboard was open. But she didn't move. Every now and then, he played with the top of her head, gently lifting, and stroking loose strands of hair. She had that comfortable tiredness that comes from physical labour followed by a large meal.

"So, you are happy, William? You do approve of the new tenants? I know they aren't really *us*, exactly, but they do seem nice, don't they?" She leant back against the chair and looked up at him, inverted.

"Of course. They'll be fine, I'm sure." He sipped from his glass. He gave a quick frown. "Funny. You didn't mention the brother is queer."

"Is he?" She turned around to look at him. "Are you sure?"

He nodded, placidly. "Certainly. Just surprised you didn't say it. Usually, you are quite the gossip."

"Cheeky! I – Am I? I didn't know. So how could I say? I mean… how do you know? He didn't tell you?"

William snorted. "No. Of course not. But I should have thought it was obvious."

"Not to me," Betty said, with a small shake of her head. "Goodness. I don't think I've ever met a homosexual before."

"I should think you have." He laughed. "Though it sounds like you'd be oblivious either way."

Chapter Ten:
Betty (Then)

She was attempting to tidy up the front yard, resting her knees on an old brown towel. Her fingers and hands were tea-stained with the pale, dried earth. She hadn't used gloves. Mother would be horrified, but as she was finally coming around to see the house that evening this was somewhat of a last-minute panic. Broken nails were the least of her concerns. First impressions were important, especially to Mum.

Betty was leaning back on her haunches with a small pile of weeds and tufts of grass beside her when Sandra came out of the front door.

"Good morning," she said. "I'm leaving by the posh exit for once." She dipped in a small courtesy. Betty smiled at her. "Another terribly chilly day." Sandra gestured, hands up to the clear blue sky.

"A trifle hot for gardening, but I have a guest tonight so best make the effort."

"Oh, anyone special?"

"Depends on your point of view. My mother. She's here for dinner – or tea, as she would say."

Sandra nodded. "That's nice. It's good to get along with your parents." She paused. "I'm off to the grocer if you need me to get anything?"

"Ah, thanks. I think I have everything. Just bracing myself for a round of not-so-subtle hints about my terribly advancing age and her lack of grandchildren. 'By the time I was your age…'" She mimicked, shaking an index finger into the air. A small clump of mud flew from her hand as she did so.

Sandra smiled. "I'm sure she means well. But you're young enough if that's what you want. My friend Franky has just had her first one, and she's almost thirty."

"She'd have kittens if I told her that!" Betty laughed, head back, and shook her head. "But I am twenty-eight next week, actually. So she's not too far from the mark. Starting to think…" She trailed off, pursed her lips together.

"You've got time," Sandra said. "And choices… oh, and what are you doing with those dandelions and bits? The flowers would go perfectly in the flat. They must be the same shade as the carpet."

"I… what do you mean?" Betty looked down to the dandelions, and the one stubborn buttercup that she had pulled.

"The flowers. I'll put them in a jam-jar or something!" She laughed at Betty's confusion. "Some crusty old man may have labelled them weeds, but I think they are rather beautiful, in their own way, don't you?"

Betty hadn't really considered it before, but perhaps she was right. She looked down to the plants she had pulled, sunny and optimistic against the grey slabs of the yard. "Perhaps I should have left them where they were…" she said, vaguely.

"Next time," Sandra said. "Maybe it would distract Mummy from the baby talk."

"Ugh. And the unpolished floors. And the cracked cistern." She put one dusty hand on her forehead with a wince. "Don't remind me."

"Sounds like I'd better let you get back to work," Sandra said, as she waved goodbye.

*

William was home punctually, just after 5:30, as promised. She was disappointed to find that he hadn't noticed her handiwork in the front yard – but then, he hadn't noticed the weeds when they were in situ, either.

"The place looks lovely. And you do, too, of course." He reassured her, then kissed her hard on the mouth and stayed close to her face as he murmured: "You always do."

He rested his head on her shoulder and they stood in an embrace. She could smell his warm skin through his cotton shirt, and feel the firm tension of his biceps as they held each other. He gave a deep, long sigh. "I am so lucky to have you," William said into her hair.

"And I'm lucky to have you." She lowered her arms, and they fell loosely around his waist, then she ran her hands across his lower back. She edged in closer until her hips pushed against him.

She felt him stiffen.

He pulled away.

"I must wash before I go out to collect Dorothy. Best rush. Don't want to keep her waiting. But I shan't mess up the bathroom, don't fret!"

"Of course," she said, to his broad shoulders, his neat waist, as he walked away.

*

She was in the kitchen when she heard a faint
knock on the sitting room door. For one moment
she panicked that her mother was here already but
then realised how ludicrous that was, as she didn't
drive and would be unlikely to have navigated the
two buses required to get there.

Betty skipped quickly to the door, barefoot,
wiping the flour from her hands onto her pinny and
trousers as she did so.

It was Sandra. Betty took in the light turquoise
of her top, and her peaked cap and skirt, both bright
green. She had never been brave enough to wear a
hat, but it looked striking on Sandra. Betty felt the
familiar creep of a red flush advancing on her chest
and neck. She was tired and dull in comparison.

"Hello," Sandra said. "I'm not staying long as I
know you're busy. It's just that I was chatting with
Rob, and I mentioned that it's your birthday soon.
We wanted to do something to thank you for how
fab you have been, and we wondered if you might
want to come for dinner? Next weekend, perhaps?"

The blush took a ferocious hold. "Wow! That…
that's such a lovely offer. We'd be delighted."

"Not, you know, odd, with us being tenants?"
Sandra cocked her head to one side.

"I wouldn't know. I've never been a landlady
before," Betty joked. "We can make our own rules."

"So, when's the big day?" Sandra asked.

"My birthday? It's Wednesday."

"OK. Friday suit you or does William like the
pub?"

"Goodness, no. Friday will be fine." The thought of William going for Friday night drinks with colleagues was amusing.

"Great. The Friday after your birthday it is. In honour of your twenty-eighth. And then you can fill me in on how it goes this evening."

"Hopefully, there won't be anything too dramatic to tell," Betty said. She resisted the temptation to cross her fingers.

"Ah, but remember. I'm a nosey bugger. I still want the details." She smiled. "Anyway, I'm going out myself, so I'd best be off."

"I like your hat," Betty blurted out, then inwardly kicked herself for the randomness of the compliment. She sounded like a child. Like the small child that Sandra thought she was.

But Sandra seemed unfazed. "Thanks. A bit on the warm side for tonight, but fashion has to overcome practicality sometimes."

Betty looked down at her pinny and dirty brown trousers. "I'm just off to change, myself," she said.

Chapter Eleven:
Betty (Then)

She could hear William, explaining her plans to change the door into a classic design 'more in keeping with the building,' as he shouldered open the front door. She was pleasantly surprised he had taken this information in, though knew he'd only be wittering away to fill the silence left by her mother.

"And we'll change the wallpaper when we can too, of course. One thing at a time."

"Not much wrong with it," Dorothy replied. "Nothing a good bit of sugar soap and elbow grease wouldn't fix, anyway."

There it was. Clearly, the cleaning had already fallen below her standards: never mind that the place had been much filthier when they had first moved in. Betty steeled herself and opened the sitting room door to meet her mother, who jumped a little. She stood in a coat, in spite of the heavy, summer air, and clutched a small bunch of pink carnations.

"Hello!" Betty overcompensated, with a wide swoop of her arms and a large grin. "Come in! I'm so happy you are finally here."

"Glad I'm here? You're the one who's been dilly-dallying. You could have had me here weeks ago." She stepped into the room, an out-of-place stiff figure in their home.

"I know Mum," she said, holding out one hand for the flowers. Dorothy started to take off her coat but kept the carnations tightly gripped, forcing her to shuffle one shoulder and shrug the sleeve off.

"I wanted you to come when we were a bit more settled."

Her mother looked around the sitting room and raised her brows.

"You've finished, have you?" she said, pointedly.

"No, not exactly. But at least we won't be having dinner amongst a mound of boxes."

"Tea," her mother corrected, automatically. "No, there is that."

Betty took her coat from her. "Shall I put those in some water?" She gestured to the carnations.

Her mother looked down as if surprised to find the flowers there. "Oh, yes. For you." She held them out.

"How lovely," William said. "Let me take them, and I'll get you both a drink at the same time. You two catch up for a moment." He swooped in and took the flowers from Mum and the coat from Betty, before either had a chance to protest.

"You sit there, Mum," she said, gesturing to William's chair. She had plumped the cushion earlier. For a fleeting moment, she wondered if she should have checked the cracks and crevices for crumbs or pennies. If there was anything amiss, Dorothy would certainly find it.

Dorothy didn't move. Feet steady and still, she took in the room with a slow turn of the shoulders and head.

"This is a nice enough room," she said. "Nice and bright." Betty was delighted but said nothing.

By Mum's standards, this was high praise. Betty took a seat on the sofa – a cast-off from William's friend Geoffrey. She had thrown a light-weight brown blanket over it, in an attempt to hide the small rip on one seam.

"You could do with better curtains, though," her mum commented. It was true, but Betty still felt a pang.

"Sit down, Mum. You're making me nervous." She attempted a joke, which was ignored, though her mother did move towards the chair.

William returned with a bottle of sweet sherry. Betty could almost feel the sticky dust on its neck.

"Where on earth did you find that?" she asked, laughing.

William smiled. "Fancy some? Or is it too early?"

She heard her mother breathe in heavily, but then she answered: "Just a drop. As long as you both are, that is."

"Definitely," William answered, shooting Betty a glance.

*

The meal went as smoothly as could be expected. The conversation mostly centred around their new cutlery and dinner sets, which Betty was using for the first time that evening. Betty thought them terribly stylish; far removed from the usual brown earthenware they ate from. These were off-white, glazed China with a gold trim, and in the centre of each piece was a small, abstract painting of something green; they disagreed on what it was. William argued that it represented an olive and a sprig, while Dorothy said it was a Bay Leaf. Betty suspected that her mother didn't know what an olive looked like, but she didn't mind and was happy as long as the topic stayed away from babies and the cost of the house.

The conversation about the dinner service in turn led to reminiscing about the wedding day. It had been simple, but lovely, and everything had gone to plan. She enjoyed reliving it and watching William's face shift and light up as they described it. She was sure his parents would have wanted something much more ostentatious, but neither of them had aspirations for big white weddings or hundreds of guests. They, too, had been happy in the end.

Dorothy had two portions of the shepherd's pie, which Betty took to be a good sign.

"We will have you around again, now, Mum. Seems silly to wait until we've done more work seeing as you've had the full 'warts and all' insight this evening. You could come for dinner in a couple of weeks if you like."

"Tea," both Dorothy and William corrected, simultaneously.

Betty jumped a little, hearing them in unison, and her mother actually laughed.

"Fast learner," she quipped.

"Thank you," he said.

"I haven't seen everything, though, have I? We didn't get to the top floor."

"I told you, Mum. There's nothing to see. It's full of boxes and cobwebs at the moment. We shan't be tackling it for some time."

Dorothy pulled down the corners of her mouth and looked at the table. Betty sensed it; the judgement. Not that she needed it – she already felt guilty each time she thought of the attic floor, jumbled, disordered, cluttered. It was probably worse than the way her mother imagined it to be. Betty rarely ventured there. She found excuses not to. Besides, that floor of the house had a peculiar smell, and it was colder than the rest. Like a different place.

"What about Friday, next week?" William asked, guiding the subject. "Always good to have guests on payday. Puts me in a generous mood."

Betty stood up and started to tidy and carry the dirty plates into the kitchen.

"No, that's when we are with Sandra, remember? I mentioned it when you were getting ready. I knew you weren't really listening." She smiled at William.

"That's an awfully long way away. Shall I not be seeing you on your birthday, then?" Dorothy asked, her voice a touch quieter than usual.

"Yes," Betty said. "I can pop to you if you like. For a cuppa."

"I don't wish to impose. Only if you're free." Dorothy sniffed.

"I should think I will be."

"And who's this Sandra? I don't recall any friends called Sandra."

"Well," Betty said, filling the sink with warm water from the taps, calling across from the kitchen to the dining area through the open double doors. "She's not exactly a friend. I mean… she is nice. And friendly. But we don't know her that well yet.

She and her… husband." She closed her eyes briefly at the lie. "They're our new tenants. Downstairs."

"I see," Dorothy said. "You think that's a good idea, do you?"

Betty leant across to look back through the doorway at her. She was lifting the corner of the tablecloth, trying to look at the wood beneath. Betty came back for more dishes and pushed her hand away. A glob of froth fell from her damp hand onto her mother's.

"What do you mean by that?" she asked, annoyed. For a moment, she thought Dorothy was going to lift the cloth again, as her soapy hand moved back over, and paused, fingers resting in a small pool of gravy.

"Mind," she said, gesturing to her hand. Dorothy moved it with a grimace and rubbed her hands together in her lap.

"Not my place to say."

"No, go on." Betty leant over and continued to load herself with dishes. "I'm asking. Why would it not be a *good idea*." She could hear her voice – pointed and shrill – but couldn't curtail it.

"If you must know, being chums with people living in the basement doesn't strike me as the cleverest of ideas."

Betty turned and tottered back towards the kitchen, irritated. She slammed the dinnerware down onto the surface and had to rescue a glass that rolled on its side, precariously. William jumped up to help, restacking the plates and putting an arm across her shoulders, briefly, with a quick squeeze.

"That's rather a snobby attitude, don't you think? The riffraff shouldn't mix with the homeowners?"

58

Dorothy huffed. "No. Don't put words in my mouth, Elizabeth. I would never say that."

"You wouldn't *say it*, but you have *implied it*." She started to drop the side plates into the soapy water, heavily, brusquely, neglecting to put on the gloves that William held out for her.

"I have done no such thing."

"Oh, Mother. Just be straight for once."

"All I am saying," Dorothy enunciated, "is to be careful mixing business with pleasure. You need their rent, I take it? To finish this great big house you've purchased. So, what do you do when these new *friends* of yours skip a week – or ask for an extension – or tell you they're struggling to make ends meet? A lot easier to stand your ground with a tenant than a friend."

Betty dropped her hands into the water. She was right, of course. She was right. There was silence, for a beat. She stood, facing the wall, hands in the sink.

After a while, she heard William reaching for a bottle of something from the cupboard and then placing more glasses on the table.

"Port, anyone?" he asked. No one answered.

"Damnit, Mother. I… I just wanted some new friends."

"I know. I do remember. It's lonely being the homemaker, isn't it?"

Betty turned towards her with a wet smile: touched, surprised.

"And watch your bloody language," Dorothy said, reaching for a glass of port.

Chapter Twelve:
Betty (Now)

It had been another restless night. She had dozed off in front of the television and when she had awoken, past midnight, she knew immediately that it was going to be a long stretch before she could sleep again. Sleep would catch her in the evening, but then evade her again at night. Briefly, she had wondered if it was morning, such was the depth of the sleep she had experienced.

The walk from the living room to bed was usually enough to awaken her, but this time she needed a trip to the bathroom first, as well. On the way back, she made herself a herbal tea and added a splash of whisky, straight into the cup, which she had in bed while reading. She had read three chapters and finished the drink before turning the lamp off – but sleep had steadfastly eluded her.

It must have been approaching 2am before she had nodded off, into a headachy, erratic sleep punctured by short, fleeting dreams, whose images were out of reach upon waking.

That morning, she had felt stiff, and old, but determined to get outside to enjoy the sunshine and shake off the discomfort of the night. With toast and marmalade, she sat at her kitchen table and made a list of tasks to complete.

She had cleaned the toilet and bathroom sink and

was about to hang her washing out at 11am when David knocked on the door of her flat. He was still wearing the same grey t-shirt and baggy tracksuit bottoms from the night before, she noted. They had not always been so loose.

"Hello, David. How are you?" She tried to sound cheery, pleased to see him. Anything to encourage him to maintain these visits.

"Did I disturb you?" he asked.

"No, no. I was listening to the wireless, that's all." She lied, fearful of scaring him away.

"No, last night," he said. "Did I keep you awake?"

It struck her then that perhaps he had. Perhaps this explained the uncomfortable, fitful sleep. Somewhere in her subconscious, she may have noted the thump of his punchbag or the banging of boxes being moved. Or maybe it was even deeper than that. She sensed him.

But she said nothing.

"Not at all. A chamomile tea and some whisky and I am out like a light. Mind you, I'm awake again at five-thirty. That's what happens with old age, I'm afraid. Were you up very late?"

"Yes. Sorry." He spoke flatly, matter of fact. But she knew him of old. He would be bothered by this. His imposition.

"Did you get everything done this time?" she asked.

"Not really… I… No. Not at all."

She smiled and started to speak, wanting so much to reassure him. She thought back to her own experience of sorting William's things. How she had put it off for weeks – perhaps months. Then she had chipped away, working on it in fits and starts, until eventually, she had spent two full days working through his things at a pace, unrelenting. Until the job was done.

"I feel like I'll never get it done," he said, his voice growing louder, cracking. She saw his pain and the accompanying shame at his emotion, so close to the surface.

"My dear boy," she said. "You must come and have a cup of tea."

"And what about whisky?" he joked.

"That too, if you like."

*

He had drunk several cups of tea, and eaten biscuits. He had even accepted her offer of a small Tupperware of quiche, to take with him for later. She could sense that he was building up to leaving, but she was worried about the prospect of him being upstairs again, alone. She pictured him, shuffling from room to room in that dusty place. Talking to no one. Hearing from no one. She wondered when he had last seen daylight, or spoken to anyone but her. This was no way for a young man to live.

A thought struck her. "Before you disappear, there is one little job you could do for me if you don't mind? Cheeky I know, but you see, I'm stiff as a board at the moment, and tormented by the thought of the weeds between the slabs, out front. Could you pull them up for me? It's not a huge job, but…" She trailed off. She was staring at him, imploring, leaning forward. She knew he would find

62

it difficult to resist.

"Of course," he said, moving to stand. He followed her, dutifully, upstairs and outside.

*

She made herself comfortable on the bench and chattered as he moved about on his hands and knees, carefully pulling up the dandelions, exactly as instructed. She started to tell him about the very first time she had done this herself.

She was used to it now, she told him. She didn't mind the weeds and the undulating surface. But when she first moved into Hummingbird House, she had been concerned to gain her mother's approval, and so had spent one afternoon yanking late buttercups and dandelions from the crevices. He smiled briefly and sat back on his haunches, while she described a young Betty and her overbearing mum. She explained how, in desperation, she had thought it essential to weed the front of the building. As if this would engender a terrific transformation to the appearance of the dilapidated house.

She stumbled in her tale, thinking of Sandra, bending down, her elegant hands, pinching a small bundle of weeds between her fingers. She faltered, unsure how to finish, but then realised David had not taken in a word for the last few minutes. He was off, locked in his own thoughts again. She changed tack and started to tell him about old wives' tales associated with dandelions, instead.

She had always intended to repave the area but had never done so. She had replaced them,

63

individually, as they cracked beyond repair: hence the hodgepodge of shades and textures. But she had never taken them up in one go, as intended. As she had told William she would.

Across the street, Betty saw April pull up in her little car. At least her eyesight had never failed her. She said nothing, worried about David's reaction. Instead, she tried to distract him – pointing at the tiniest of emerging plants with her toe. She continued with her inane chatter as the young woman approached, finally giving her a broad smile in the hope of ensuring that she stopped.

How she would love these two to be friends.

She saw him flinch as April greeted them; the colour rising in his cheeks. He froze. His eyes flicked to the side, as he listened. "How do?" was all he said.

Betty chattered to April, hoping to keep her for longer, hoping for some change in David. A thawing. But it didn't happen. He didn't speak at all when she said her goodbyes. What would April think of him? Rude, boorish, no doubt. So far from the truth.

Betty knew she needed a far more elaborate plan if she wanted to bring him out of his shell.

Chapter Thirteen
Betty (Then)

She knew it was foolish, but Betty had spent all week mulling over what to wear. Now it was Friday, and she still wasn't entirely sure. Staring at her wardrobe, she couldn't help but notice how bland and uniform it was. The majority of her clothes seemed to be brown. Autumnal at best. She had a row of cigarette pants in black, and shades of brown. A couple of dresses. A row of blouses and tops, mostly plain cream or brown. Unlike Sandra, with her peacock hues and bold, black and white prints.

Betty had decided on her orange mini-skirt – the only mini she owned – as Sandra had once admired it, and she loved the way it cut at exactly the right point to flatter her thighs. She felt a tingle of butterflies each time she wore it, which wasn't often, as it required some nerve. But she was unhappy with every top she considered. In the end, she settled for plain white. She glanced at her reflection in the full-length mirror which was propped up against the bedroom wall. It was an unflattering angle, looming upwards to show the tops of her thighs and her double chin, but even so, she looked presentable.

They were due downstairs for half past six, but by 4:30 Betty found herself sitting in front of her dressing-table mirror, attempting to mould her ponytail into something more fashionable, through teasing and backcombing. After twenty minutes or so, she had managed to manipulate it into being quite presentable, and then she lacquered it into place with a much-neglected bottle of hairspray. The surface of her table turned tacky; the air thick. But it did the job.

She was dressed; hair done, but sweating and uncomfortable. She couldn't face putting any makeup on. The warm summer air was heavy and still. Besides, her face had caught the sun when she had been gardening, and walking through the park to town. She rather liked the few freckles that dotted her nose.

In the kitchen, she poured herself a lemonade and then sat at the dining table, listening to the news on her transistor radio, and wondering how it was that time could move so slowly on occasions such as these. It was only 5pm. Just as she was considering completing more housework, purely to pass the time, she caught sight of the present her mother had given her on her birthday. Dorothy hadn't wanted her to open it at the time, gruffly telling her she wasn't a child, and she was sure Betty could wait until she was back at home. Since then, it had sat on the sideboard, untouched.

She suspected it to be a pack of tea towels.

She moved over to it, and picked it up, noting the old creases in the wrapping paper where her mother had ironed and then reused it. It was covered, somewhat incongruously, in a pattern of bright red apples. A childish print. She pulled apart the tiny squares of Sellotape to reveal a large, lightweight scarf, decorated in small abstract flowers, in shades of pink, yellow and orange.

She lifted it up to admire the print, and layers of the delicate fabric fell to the table before her. This was like nothing her mother had ever bought her before. It was modern. It was frivolous. Impractical.

It was beautiful.

She took the scarf and tied it loosely around her neck – the perfect accompaniment to finish her outfit.

*

Betty managed to pass the next hour or so by flipping through cookbooks, considering what she might make if the night was a success and Sandra and Robert ever paid a return visit. After a little while, she actually became quite captivated by the recipes. She had received her Good Housekeeping book when they married – secretly disappointed not to have had Julia Child instead – and at the time she had thought she would probably never open it. Yet, as an endless sea of evening meals rolled in front of her, she was beginning to realise that she probably needed to expand her repertoire. Unless she was going to rotate the same seven dishes each week, as her mother did, of course.

Besides, learning to cook might be another way to fill the hours once the more attainable jobs in the house had been completed. This was a prospect that didn't seem too far away. They would be moving on to chores and adjustments that she couldn't do herself, within the next month, perhaps. What on earth would she do with her time then?

"*Have a baby, of course*," her mother's voice instantly snapped in her head. She shook the thought away, tangled as it was with questions and worries. Perhaps tackling the top floor of the house was a more realistic prospect.

At around ten to six, William arrived home, suit jacket over one arm, tie and collar loosened. His cheeks were flushed and his hair ruffled. She stood and went straight to him, wrapping her arms around his waist, taking in the warm smell of him, sensing the weight of the case that he carried.

"You poor dear," she said. "What a day to have to spend hours cooped up in an office." She kissed his cheek and then buried her face in his shoulder, as she was wont to do. He gave a quick peck to the top of her head and then pulled back, holding her at arm's length. He looked at her, apparently bemused.

"What is it?" she asked.

"I'm just admiring you. And I don't want to ruin this… froo-froo thingamabob you've manifested on your head."

"Manifested? And it's called a ponytail, silly. She dropped her hands to her sides and then gave an exaggerated twirl. "Do you like it?"

"I do. I do. It's rather foxy." He winked.

She giggled. "You had better freshen up. Don't want our new tenants to think I've married beneath myself." She pointed towards the bathroom.

He gave an exaggerated gasp. "Oh no, we'll be rumbled!"

*

At half past six on the dot, William gave a quick tap on the door of the basement flat. Robert opened swiftly, barefoot, smiling, with his green paisley-print shirt unbuttoned to reveal most of his torso. Betty felt the pink rising on her neck, towards her chin and cheeks, as she took in the thick coils of his black chest hair.

The two men shook hands enthusiastically, and it struck her again how William seemed unfazed by anything and everyone. Odd, she felt, given that of the two of them, he was the one who had never experienced genuine financial hardship or lived in a troublesome neighbourhood. His life was a neat little box of tidiness and comfort. His extended family was cold and well-to-do, the school he had attended was impeccable. Surely she should be the more worldly-wise of the two?

But then, he was male. He had probably been privy to all sorts of things that she was unaware of. He had that easy confidence that can come with wealth and manhood.

Robert ushered them in, taking Betty's bottle of wine enthusiastically but then placing it down on the sideboard. There was a small jam-jar of buttercups next to it.

"Sandy is in the bedroom. She'll be out in a tick. Do you fancy a drink? I mean, a *drink* drink. She's gotten me into these Tom Collins things lately…" He whistled dramatically, then crossed his eyes. "Man, they are go-ood." He pretended to stagger into her.

"Umm… I…" Betty mumbled. William placed an arm around her shoulder. "I'm not sure—" she continued.

69

"Sounds delightful," William said. He gave her a small squeeze.

"Fab," Robert said as he made his way towards the kitchenette at the back. Laid out already was a chopping board laden with lemon and a beautiful orange glass pitcher.

"Gin," William mouthed to her.

Again, she had that feeling of being a young child in a crowd of adults, who each knew what they were doing, with shared jokes and intimacies, and all spoke the same language, while she floundered and played dress-up amongst them. Crashing disappointment enveloped her as she realised this evening might not be at all like she had hoped. It could be more stressful than fun.

But then Sandra appeared, pulling back the sliding door that led to the bedroom at the front of the flat, and Betty was back in the room again.

Chapter Fourteen
Betty (Then)

The drink was cold and strong. Betty and William were on the sofa. Sandra sat next to Robert in his chair, perched on the arm of it, one leg gently draped over his. She held her glass up in the air, elbow bent, wrist loose. She wore a light cotton dress in pale blue, with white decorations down the centre and a Peter Pan collar. Everything about her was confident and casual.

The men were discussing the commute to and from work – William explaining how he usually walked, as he could cut through the park, and he enjoyed the air. Robert took the bus but had a yearning for a motorbike. Sandra tussled his hair and rolled her eyes when he spoke about it.

Before she knew it, Betty had finished her drink. She was the first to do so. Robert jumped up without comment and took her glass, pouring her another as he started to ask William about his car.

"Goodness don't start him on that topic," Betty said. "He can talk the hind legs off a donkey when it comes to his precious Vauxhall Viva." It was the first time she had spoken.

"Now, now, I promise I won't bore you, except to say you're welcome to come for a spin sometime. See what you think. She's a nippy little thing."

"I will definitely take you up on that."

"What about you, Sandra, where do you work?" William asked.

"I'm lucky. I share a studio space with a friend, Helen. I mean, it's basically an old garage that we have put some rugs in," she said, flippantly, "But it's fine for nine or ten months of the year. I give it a wide berth around January. Even I am not that dedicated. I do sketches and preparatory work then, if I don't have a commission. Lazy, really. But most of the time, it gives me space to be super messy and wild."

"Is that one of yours?" Betty pointed to a large oil painting on the facing wall. It looked to be of three naked figures, in an archway, but she was nervous to comment specifically as she wasn't fully certain what it depicted. It was bright cerise and yellow.

"Well spotted. That is one I did several years ago. Robert has a soft spot for it, though every time I look at it, all I can see is how the perspective is a bit off on the bloke at the front."

Robert was grinning. "I love it. My Old Lady is so talented, man."

"It's very powerful," William said, nodding as he stared at it. He turned to Sandra. "But you have another job, too, don't you? I thought Betty said that you served customers."

"Ha! No, not exactly. I do work with… the public."

Robert slapped his thigh. "Oh yes, some of her job is very public!"

Sandra rolled her eyes. "That joke doesn't even make sense." She turned towards William and leant forward slightly, her wrists crossed, now empty glass dangling limply. "Are you easily shocked, William?"

"I should say not." He held her gaze.

"Good. Because some people do find my side-line quite shocking."

"Then perhaps –" he held his glass up, "you should tell us after another drink." His voice was low and teasing. Betty found the exchange odd, and unsettling, though she wasn't sure why.

"Yes! More drinks," Robert said, standing. Sandra slipped into the empty space on his chair.

"Be a darling and put the kettle on the stove, would you, while you are over there? For the spaghetti."

"Spaghetti!" Betty said. "I've never tried it."

"Really? You'll love it. We've even got some red wine, too."

*

As they went to the table, Betty discovered an envelope with her name on marking one of the places. Surprised, felt herself step backwards when she saw it. Robert was delighted by her reaction, but in fact, she had assumed it was something awful. A letter of complaint. A bill of some kind. That made no sense, of course. She didn't know why her mind automatically strayed to the negative.

"Open it!" Robert cried.

"Happy birthday," Sandra said, at almost the same time. Of course – a birthday card.

Betty sat down and unpeeled the glue from the back of the envelope. It felt light, and floppy, and clearly didn't contain a conventional card.

73

Inside was a piece of rough paper – edges torn and frayed. In the centre was a small, detailed sketch of a hummingbird. It was in pen and ink, mostly black, but with a few strong, sweeping brushstrokes of turquoise and emerald blue, across the wing and chest. It was stunning.

"It's… it's beautiful," she said.

Betty turned to William, to show him, but he was already close by, standing close to her shoulder. Her eyes were pricking again, and she felt overwhelmed by all the people, watching, surrounding her.

"A beautiful gift for a beautiful lady," he said.

*

Betty struggled to eat the spaghetti at first. After several failed attempts to wrap it around her fork, Robert stood and got her a knife, without comment. She felt the usual glow as her blushes ascended from her chest to her neck. She caught William's eye.

"Do you know, I could do with a knife myself if you don't mind? I'm struggling a bit here." Betty appreciated the thought, though he had been making a far better job of it than she had. Sandra stood and collected another bottle of wine along with the cutlery.

"Right," said William. "I think it's about time you spared us from our misery. What *is* it that you do for a living, Sandra?"

"Damn it. I rather hoped you'd forgotten about that."

"'Fraid not. As your landlord, I demand to know."

"Ok, perhaps I should give this some context."

Robert leant back in his chair, gleefully rubbing his hands on his thighs.

"I went to a rather prestigious ladies' school. I know, I know. You'd never tell. Anyway, my mother was rather keen on the idea of my going to university. She fancied herself as a bit of an intellectual and wanted to live vicariously through me."

"How wonderful," Betty said. "I would have loved that."

Sandra frowned. "Quite. Anyway, I surprised everyone by getting a rather glorious set of exam results, in spite of being – how shall I put it? – a bit of a scamp. But then I buggered off to art college."

"And that's not what she had in mind?" William asked, chopping up his pasta.

"Not exactly. She was thinking more along the lines of Classics, I gather. So, she wasn't too pleased with my choice of HCA."

"A good College, though, I believe. Well done, you," William said.

"HCA? What's that?" Betty asked.

"Hornsey College of Art," she answered. "It was great fun. Loved every minute of it – there was something hugely liberating about being so far away from home, and around like-minded souls, even if the curriculum was still somewhat stuffy for my liking." She ran a finger slowly around the edge of her glass as she spoke. "They wouldn't have thought much of this stuff." She waved her hand vaguely towards the painting.

"Ray Davies was there. Tell them, Sandy."

"Was he? Wow. Were you friends?" Betty asked.

It was William's turn to be confused. "Is he an artist?"

Betty laughed and touched his arm. "He's a singer in The Kinks, isn't he?" She turned to Robert, who nodded enthusiastically, though William continued to shake his head, face blank. "You know… All Day and All of the Night? They are a pop group, darling."

"Ah, no. I can't say it rings any bells."

"I'll put their LP on!" Robert said, making to stand.

"Hang on… We were just hearing about how Sandy became the black sheep of the family. We've not yet learnt what her illicit occupation is."

"After art college I moved back home but I couldn't settle. East Sussex seemed so dull and staid. And mother had made it clear that if I was to continue staying with them, I needed a *proper* job. I was a waitress at the time. She was mortified. So, I decided to make my way here. And that's when I met Robert."

"So, you're not a waitress now, then?" Betty asked, egging her along.

"No. I'm a model."

"A model?"

"Yes, at the local art school. It's good money, and I just drift off, thinking of what I will paint that evening, myself. Or what to cook for dinner."

"I don't understand… why is modelling so shocking? In this day and age, I wouldn't think it held such a stigma," Betty said.

"That depends on your point of view. I'm a life model. I pose in the nude."

*

After the meal, the men went out into the garden. Betty and Sandra cleared the table, and Betty was about to start washing the dishes when Sandra told her she was planning to leave everything until the next day.

"Sit on the sofa and have some more wine," she told her.

"I… I couldn't have a cup of tea, could I? I'll have more later, but I'm not really used to red wine and that plus the spicy food has made me feel a bit woozy."

"Of course. But… spicy food? It wasn't spicy." She was filling the kettle already.

"It didn't have garlic in it? I could have sworn I could taste garlic. And onions."

Sandra snorted. "You are a funny thing. Spicy. Yes, yes, it did."

"I did like it, though. Honestly. I am hoping to widen the range of meals we eat – it's all rather dull and English in our house, and yet neither of us is overly fussy. In fact, William loves his food. He'll try pretty much anything. You don't – you wouldn't have any good recipe books I could borrow, would you?"

"Yes, I'm sure we do. I'll drop something around tomorrow."

The kettle boiled, and Sandra set about making her tea, as well as placing a couple of biscuits on a side plate and topping up her own red wine. She placed everything on the table, and they remained in the kitchen area.

"So, you didn't go to university, Betty?"

"Me? Goodness no. I did pass the Eleven Plus. Went to grammar school. My mum now blames every little idiosyncrasy I have on 'that bloody school'… Apparently, it turned me into some pretentious tearaway. She's forever telling me I've got pretentions. Of course, it's gone now. I think it merged with the secondary modern. The building's been knocked down, anyway. It was a horrible old place – freezing, always smelt funny. Cracked windows. But I didn't mind. I loved school."

"So, what did you do when you left school?"

"I wanted to be a teacher, but Mum thought that was a ludicrous idea." She looked up to Sandra, who raised her glass in a toast in response. "So, I went to work for Bloomer's Bakeries. You know? But in the office. I was essentially a secretary, but by the time I left, they had me helping with payroll and things. The Office Manager gave me a bit of a promotion and sort of took me under their wing. I had a fab time there." She took a sip of tea. "I miss it." It was only as she said the words that she realised this was true. She did miss it. She thought of those days with affection. Strangely, rather than causing her stress, she had found she had thrived on the extra responsibility they had given her. And quite frankly, she had not found any of it difficult.

"So why did you leave, then? It sounds perfect."

"I only left at the start of the year. Because we were getting married."

"I see. But if you'd stayed, wouldn't that have helped towards the costs of doing this place up? Sorry. Sorry. Be quiet, Sandra. You nosey git."

"Yes though, you're right. And we did discuss it. But William's parents, and my mum, they were both pretty adamant that a married woman should be at home. I had mixed feelings. William's very easy-going, so he wouldn't have minded if I had wanted to stay there, but he did prefer the idea of looking after me and avoiding conflict with his mother-in-law. And when I saw the house, I figured I could use my time as productively by helping to decorate and dress it."

Sandra frowned but didn't answer.

"Do you think you'll ever work again at some point? I mean, after kids, instead of kids, whatever."

"Instead of kids?"

"If you decide not to have them."

"I – I'm pretty sure we will, I mean, I know I'm getting older, but we have only just married, so…" she trailed off.

"Sorry. No offence. Nosey git strikes again. I was just thinking you seemed very animated when you were talking about work. And you don't *have* to have children. I don't imagine I will."

"Really?" Betty asked, surprised. "You're younger than me. Perhaps in a couple of years."

"Hmmm." Sandra shrugged.

"Doesn't Robert want children?"

"Robert?" She threw her head back, with a forced laugh.

The men came back into the basement in a bubble of laughter and noise.

"Right. It's time for some music!" Robert said, his voice louder than necessary.

"Let's go over to the comfy seats," Sandra said. "And it's about time you had another glass of wine."

"Ugh," Betty answered. "I know it's probably not the thing to say but is there any chance of my rosé? I am not used to this red stuff, and it was making me a bit headachy."

"You can have anything you want," Sandra answered. "You're my guest tonight." She winked at her, then walked over to the kitchenette, and Betty sat back comfortably on the sofa, as Robert placed The Kinks on the record player.

Chapter Fifteen
Betty (Then)

It was 11:30 before Betty and William made their way back upstairs. He had opened two more buttons on his shirt and rolled up his sleeves. She was carrying her shoes in one hand, her new scarf tied loosely around her head – Sandra's work. She recalled how she had leant in, her face so close to Betty's that she could feel Sandra's breath on her cheek; smell the vanilla tones of her perfume.

They danced, all of them, together. Sometimes the two women holding hands, jumping, banging into one another and laughing. Other times, they danced in pairs, switching partners every few minutes, until even the men had danced together. She had been tickled at the sight of William, whom she had never really seen dancing before. Her feet were grubby and the armholes of her top had rubbed and scratched her skin from the friction, but she didn't care. She didn't care.

She followed William, who made his way straight upstairs to the first floor, his feet hitting each step heavily, his right hand pulling the banisters to propel him upwards or to steady himself, perhaps. His body was languid and loose: her beautiful man. He turned towards her as they reached the bedroom door, grinning.

Then he leant forward and kissed her with the passion she had longed for. Hard, strong, but tender. And she kissed him back with the fierce intensity of five months of longing. Twenty-eight years of chastity.

And they made love for the first time.

Chapter Sixteen
Betty (Now)

A few days later, Betty sent a text message to Jonty, inviting him to come downstairs and out into the garden for cake. Years ago, she had considered some sort of intercom system between the flats, but technology moved on apace before she had time to install one. It would be wasted, now. Mobile phones had been a revelation to her. While she was not one to carry it every moment of the day, she did enjoy the fact she could stay in touch so easily, and check the weather forecast when she liked.

She tried not to message the tenants too often, as she knew it could be an imposition. In most cases, she used to phone to make announcements: changes to the rubbish collection day; oil deliveries; that sort of thing. But somehow it was different with Jonty, who had been there the longest, who she knew best, and who always relished a natter. She could hear the mellow tones of conversation upstairs, so knew he was in, and it wasn't unheard of for them to have a little gossip together, periodically.

Cake?? I'm there! Give me ten min.

It was cloudy, but she was glad of it. She didn't enjoy the heat these days, and her flat didn't have the best ventilation. It was still warm enough to brave the elements. She liked any excuse to go outside. Within minutes, she had plated up some slices of lemon cake and made a full pot of tea, unsure if Ben would be joining them. No matter either way, Jonty would easily be persuaded to take some cake with him when he left. As it happened, Jonty arrived five minutes later, alone.

"Ugh, he's in the middle of some damn essay so I was glad of the invite, I can tell you. Every five mins he's there asking me if what he's written about Rodin makes sense. As if I bloody know? The only art critic I know is Grayson Perry. Apparently, suggesting we watch him on TV as homework is 'flippant'."

Betty smiled, knowing full well how much these two men doted on one another.

"It's supposed to be five thousand words. He told me he's halfway through, but he's already written six. He keeps reading bits aloud to me. Quoting. Why he thinks I'll be a help, I've no idea."

"I bet you understand more than you let on. You have it in your genes." She waggled a finger at him, dramatically, then turned back to get the crockery together. "How much longer 'til Ben finishes his degree, now? Surely, he's almost there." She was placing items on the tray as she spoke.

"You'd bloody think so, wouldn't you?" he said. "But the OU takes years. He's been at it for what feels like *decades*… But no. To be truthful, I think he's got about another eighteen months." He paused, picking up the teapot, automatically. "Don't get me wrong, he's done brilliantly. It's a huge sort of validation for him, as his grades have been astronomical. Rightly or wrongly, he always felt somehow inferior by not having been to university.

Like he needed to prove his intellect in other ways. But honestly, if you ever hear me encouraging him in one of his hair-brained schemes again, then please remind me of the trauma I'm going through now."

"I shall do no such thing," Betty replied, leading the way outside. "Everyone needs someone to encourage them sometimes. And that young man has been a wonderful support to you at other times, has he not?" They reached the old wooden furniture that sat in the garden. It needed re-staining, she noted, with a sigh. "Speaking of which, that's sort of why I wanted to chat with you."

"Betty, I love you. But if you're thinking of doing a History of Art degree, you're on your own, love."

"Ha!" she said. "Now, that's an idea…" She started to pour the tea. There was a small part of her did regret never returning to her studies, but it was too late now. When she spoke again, her voice was soft and low. "No. It's not so much me that needs the support, but one of our lovely neighbours. Top floor." She pointed upwards, and looked, half expecting to see David's face at the window. Of course, he wasn't there. The curtains were closed.

"Ah, yes. He's not looking his best, is he? Poor bugger."

"Quite," she said. "I'm trying to engineer some means of forcing him to shake it off. A bit of normality. A project, perhaps… I wondered if you had any ideas? You love a bit of scheming, I know." He pursed his lips as if offended. "Plus, I'd love to see him getting to know young April, too. It couldn't do any harm."

"You little matchmaker, you." Jonty teased, leaning forward to pour the tea. She watched as a small drop fell and was quickly absorbed into the wood, staining it a deep brown, temporarily.

"Not so. I just have a feeling they could be a help to one another."

"Dai and April. Hmmm… The newcomer and the hermit… I tell you what, Betty. I feel a barbecue coming on." He leant forward to pick up a slice of cake. "Leave it with me."

Chapter Seventeen
Betty (Then)

The day after the dinner party, Betty had found her emotions, and her stomach, swooping and dropping throughout the day. At some points, she felt elated and light-headed, giggly, whereas at others she was overcome with the sense that perhaps she had made an imbecile of herself or been an embarrassment. It reminded her of her adolescence – that erratic, unsettling pendulum of emotions and self-doubt.

When she was younger – nineteen, twenty, she used to go out each Friday night with her friend Susan. They had known each other since school and had a closeness built upon shared memories. The type of comfort that grows when you have known someone for a long time, and they have seen the worst of you, as well as the best.

Betty used to go to Susan's house and sit on the edge of her bed as she got ready, sometimes using a little of Susan's face powder or a dab of her perfume. Her own mother did not approve of these things, and Betty found it not worth the argument that would ensure if she tried. She would usually sleep over at Susan's too, as she had little curfew. They would traipse between local pubs, where they sat together and gossip, and buy drinks on a tight budget. Occasionally, they would stay out even later and dance, then top and tail in Susan's single bed, giggling and whispering with ringing ears and the smell of cigarette smoke in their hair. But it had been a long time since they had done that – not since Susan had met James.

By 6pm, Betty found herself tearful and nauseated, standing in the bathroom, examining her bloated face in the mirror. The harsh, artificial light did not help. Her eyes were bloodshot. The lids heavy.

William assured her this was all normal.

"It's a hangover," he said. "That's all. I've had a few hefty ones myself when I was younger."

"I've had them too," she answered. "But not like this. Maybe red wine doesn't agree with me."

"It is heavy stuff if you aren't used to it. But you did also mix your drinks, darling. Give it time. You'll be fine." He tousled her hair, and she pulled away. He turned her around to face him and she leant into his shoulder. "You had… a big night."

She made to pull away because she wanted to see his face, but he held her tight, and she relaxed into him again. They stayed together for a moment until she felt too smothered and hot. She wriggled free.

"I'm going to have a big wash and put my nightie on," she said. "I don't care how early it is."

"You do that," he said. "And I'll make a pot of tea."

She shut the bathroom door behind him, wondering if there would be more spots of blood in her underwear, as there had been that morning.

*

It was late afternoon, three days later, before Sandra came around with her cookbooks, as promised. In the intervening period, Betty had convinced herself that Sandra and Robert were avoiding them. That they had hated the evening. That she had made a fool of herself. At moments, this dread swelled into a state of panic, that they would be moving out. They hated her.

She had seen no one else, bar William, and it had been difficult not to dwell. Flashes of herself stumbling as she danced, of not understanding their references to pop culture, and not being able to manage the spaghetti, would all pop into view, frequently, and undesired.

It transpired that Sandra had also suffered from a sore head the next day, and then had been working.

"Which side of the easel?" Betty asked while she fetched the lemonade from the fridge.

"Very funny. But a lady doesn't share these things," Sandra replied, with an exaggerated sniff. "Although, I'm so glad you weren't bothered by my work. I mean, it's not like I'm on the game or something. But I know Robert's parents were horrified when he mentioned it to them. So, I thought with you two… Not that you are like his parents exactly. God, no."

"No, I don't really give a monkey's, I must say. And you'll have got the measure of William by now. Very little fazes him."

"Ugh." Sandra coughed on her lemonade. "Sorry. I— thank goodness he's so accepting! I couldn't believe it when Rob told me he'd smoked pot in front of him. I could have killed him."

Betty hesitated, unsure how to respond to this.

"I— did he? William didn't say."

"Oops. Foot in mouth. Let's pretend I didn't mention that, shall we?" She took the glass to her mouth again and wiggled her eyebrows mischievously at her. "Betty, look at you. You're blushing again. You do make me laugh. You're not exactly worldly, are you?"

"You will have to educate me, then," Betty said.

"Corrupt you, do you mean?" She put her glass down. "Anyway, we can start with cuisine. I have for you a combination of basic, traditional platters, a smattering of French cookery, and even some spicy offerings."

"Good." Betty leant forward and picked up the books from the table. "Is your spaghetti in here, somewhere?"

"I even marked the page for you," Sandra replied, with a nod.

"Well, then. I propose a return visit. I will cook for you. In a week or two?"

"Fab. But maybe less wine this time."

*

Over an hour later, Sandra was still there. The two women were huddled close at the dining table, while she showed Betty her favourite recipes: Chicken Kiev; savoury pancakes; blue cheese dressing for salad. Betty was reminded of those evenings with Susan: of the joy of female intimacy and idle chatter. No real direction. No pressures, or judgement.

It all sounded enticing and exotic. Betty was furiously noting down Sandra's commentary and slipping pieces of paper in between the relevant pages. ("I usually double the paprika in that... I find a pinch of caster sugar helps...")

She was content. Relaxed. She had just put the kettle onto the hob for tea when there was a ferocious, urgent banging on the front door. She glanced at the clock, thinking perhaps that it was William – that something was wrong with him. But it was too early. Besides, of course, he had a key.

Betty and Sandra both froze momentarily and looked at one another. The banging resumed. Sandra was the first to stand, and Betty followed behind, holding onto the back of her blouse, pinched between finger and thumb, as the hammering continued. Whatever it was, this could not be good news.

As they went out into the hallway, the dark shape of a single figure could be seen, partially slumped against the bubbled glass. Sandra fumbled with the latch of the door, the spring of the catch snapping up and down where her hand repeatedly lost its grip. Betty moved forward and pushed her fingers away gently, opening it with one confident movement.

Nigel stumbled through the open doorway and fell, heavily, down onto one knee; a hand went to the floor, and the other slid down the front door. His trousers were torn on one leg from thigh to calf, revealing a knee, scuffed and raw. The left side of his face was puffed, pink, with a bright blue tinge about his upper cheek. And his bottom lip was red, split, and swollen as soft fruit.

Chapter Eighteen
Betty (Now)

"It's Dai," April said. "I think he's fainted."

She had rushed out to where Betty and Jonty were sitting, drinking tea, outside. The words were out of her mouth before her body had even breached the doorway. It took a moment for Betty to register what April had said. Jonty was quicker off the mark.

"What! Where?" he asked.

"Outside my flat. He's still there –"

He was gone in a flash. Betty felt unable to respond, for some reason. She and April both stood, slack-jawed and silent, as the sound of Jonty's heavy steps could be heard racing up the staircase, two at a time. This was unreal. Flashes of previous faints and accidents flickered before her: William, when he fell from a step ladder; Nigel, appearing in her doorway; her mother, lying on the floor of the kitchen, eyes closed, and knee bent at an unnatural angle.

After a beat, Betty noted that April's legs had a visible tremor. The poor girl.

"Goodness. Can I get you anything?" she asked. "Do you need to sit down?"

But April declined with a fierce shake of the head, and, inevitably but reluctantly, the two women turned together to make their way back into the house, fearful but anxious to discover what awaited them.

By the time they reached April's front door – Betty bringing up the rear – David was propped up against the wall: awake, groggy, pale. Jonty sat beside him on his haunches. There was no blood. There were no distorted limbs. Jonty had one arm loosely about David's shoulders. The other stroking David's bare forearm.

"Easy does it, fella. That'll do. You've been burning the candle at both ends, I should imagine. Eh? A cup of tea and a good sleep will do you the world of good. You've given us all a good shock, eh? And yourself I should imagine." Jonty was murmuring away, a lullaby of kindness and platitudes.

April went to squeeze by into the flat, offering water, which David declined. "No! No water." It was the only thing he had said so far. But then was even more assertive about the prospect of the ambulance offered next, as Betty knew he would be. There could only be bad memories associated with hospitals and doctors. And he was not one to make a fuss.

He pulled and pushed himself up to a standing position and leant against the door frame, tapping gently at his cheek, as it began to swell, into a small but noticeable spongy mound. With each movement he made, the three bystanders flinched and lifted their hands up, as if to catch him, in a reflex. But he kept his balance.

"Upstairs?" Jonty asked. Dai nodded.

The little group made their way carefully up the next flight of stairs. Dai was draped across Jonty's shoulders, April leading the way. Betty watched them, ahead of her. For a moment, she felt overwhelmed with emotion. The kindness and tenderness were too much to bear.

By the time she rounded the corner on the top floor, April had opened the door to David's flat. Betty flinched, wondering how he would feel – this fiercely private man, exposed and vulnerable. In the space outside the flat were mounds of boxes, bulging and torn in places, as well as suitcases, tatty, dented. Betty saw Doreen's old television. Her tabletop mirror. A single shoe, as if kicked off from a dance, resting on its side – soles grimy and worn. It reminded her of the way the space had been, all those years ago, when she and William had first moved into the house, and they had used it as an enormous, disorganised attic. Except this was a living space. A home.

April continued ahead, carefully moving a pair of boots from their path, and flicking on the corridor light. David was picking up a pace, clearly keen to be in bed and have the incident over with.

*

Thirty minutes later, Betty was sitting in Jonty and Ben's flat, cradling a cup of chamomile tea. For once, a tenant was waiting on her. It was a pleasant change, she realised. She was vaguely aware of him, flitting around the space – tidying away newspapers and opening windows. She allowed herself to fall down into a fugue of sorts: somewhat dissociated. Black. She almost enjoyed it. She was in a trance.

Eventually, Jonty came and sat next to her on the

low sofa. He had oily, black coffee in a squat mug. She could smell it, entwined with the spiced aftershave he always wore.

"I thought he'd faint again when April went to go in old Doreen's room," Jonty stated.

"Quite… to be… to be completely honest, I don't think I could have borne it myself, either. To see in there, I mean. I've not been in that room … since she passed. Not today, I couldn't bear it today. Not after seeing him like that, as well." She paused. "Oh dear. The whole thing is extraordinarily painful."

Jonty nodded and looked down at his cup; took a sip of his too-hot coffee.

"You… You OK, then?" he asked, after a beat.

"Oh yes," she answered. "And either way, it's not about me. We must focus on poor David at the moment."

"Yes. I shall make sure to speak to Paul when he returns. He will be mortified not to have been here. But you seemed a bit quiet, that's all. But as long as you're OK."

"When you get to my age, sadly, you get to witness far too many accidents and illnesses. What's shocking is the fact that you still don't expect them. That it still comes as a surprise, when something happens to someone you know."

The double doors into the bedroom at the front of the flat were open, as they usually were. Presumably, this gave more light. Betty watched as Oxo the cat jumped up and carefully navigated his way through the small gap in the open bay window, and then strutted through the bedroom towards them.

"I guess. But you can't live your whole life waiting for things to go wrong. If you did, you'd be in a state of permanent fear. And you couldn't get anything else done," Jonty said. "Like Mum. My Mum, I mean. When she moved to her new place… the very first week she had an argument with the young bloke across the road. I'd never met him, and she'd only been there five minutes, and there she is telling me how she'd bashed on his door because he'd put the rubbish out in a loose bin bag and hadn't separated out his recycling – two cardinal sins! And there she goes banging away before eight in the morning and had some fantastic run-in. I was mortified. Her description of him – even I'd be bloody scared. And that was just one example. She's always sticking her nose in and wandering about rowing with people… And then she tripped on that f- flipping curb and refused to use the crutches."

Betty turned to him. She couldn't help but smile at these tales. She pictured his mother, barging around the village knocking on doors and complaining about things in the corner shop. Oxo appeared at her feet then, his heavy purr cutting through the air as he rubbed against her legs.

"… And there was a few a months – genuinely – when I thought I might have to move to be with her. Or move her somewhere else. If she'd let me – which is unlikely." He gave a sardonic laugh and shook his head.

"So, what changed your mind?" Betty asked.

"It was partly Ben. He always relishes the phone calls we have with her. He makes me see that she's basically just having fun. He sort of re-frames my fears into an adventure. He's been chipping away

96

every time I am mortified. Plus, she wore me down because it was all so bloody relentless. And then on one of those visits to her, last year or maybe the year before, it suddenly struck me that he was right. Ben. She was enjoying herself. And that's the way she is. Always had been. Who am I to interfere? And what help is it, me fretting constantly, from afar? You know, it was genuinely making me sick. It affected my sleep, for a while."

"I didn't realise. She wouldn't want that, I'm sure." Betty said. "You're not worried about her upsetting the neighbours, anymore?"

"Worried?" He looked up at her and leant in. "Last time I was there, that bloke popped around with some jam for her. That his granny had made."

Jonty got up and indicated to her mug with a nod.

"No more, thank you. I only usually have this at bedtime," she said.

Jonty was right, of course. Worrying gets you nowhere. She wasn't one to be maudlin or anxious; at, least, not these days. As she had said, you get to witness far too many accidents and illnesses by her age. This was true. But she couldn't help noting the one thing she had left out. Not just accidents. Illnesses. But also attacks.

Chapter Nineteen
Betty (Then)

They managed to help Nigel to his feet. He seemed more concerned about closing the door than speaking. Sandra was asking him what had happened, urgently, while trying to grab him to get a closer look at him, but he batted her away, saying nothing but 'wait' and 'no' repeatedly.

He slammed the door so hard that it rattled and then swung back open. He swore, pushing it again, firmly, with both hands, one loud sob tearing out of him as he succeeded. Betty's fingers trembled as she placed the chain on the door. When she turned back, she found that Sandra was holding his arm, and he had leant into her; she staggered, attempting to take his weight, as he stooped and made to rest his head upon her shoulder. Betty moved onto the other side of him to share the load, and they attempted to shuffle as a slow train into the sitting room.

They placed him on the sofa and Sandra immediately went to remove his shoes while Betty stood by helplessly, unsure what to do next. If only they had a telephone, they could have called William. He would have known what to do.

"Betty. Cushion," Sandra said in a sharp whisper, indicating the cushion on William's chair with a brisk flick of the head. Betty took it and placed it under his head as he settled down on his side, taking the full length of the sofa. He groaned, but still did not speak. The lack of words filled the room oppressively. Sandra attempted to examine his leg, but he was turned over onto it, curled up slightly, his injuries buried; disguised beneath long limbs and torn fabric.

Instead, Sandra moved to the other end of the sofa to stroke his hair away from his forehead.

"Could you get something? A flannel, maybe?" Sandra asked Betty. A flannel. Towels. Water. Of course. Betty felt foolish and inept, but was glad, at least, to now have a role to play.

Nigel moaned.

"Sshh," Sandra said. "It's OK, now. You're safe."

Betty went into the kitchen and grabbed a large ceramic bowl. She ran the tap until it was warm and filled it, finding a clean tea towel in the drawer. She took this into the sitting room and placed it next to Sandra, who hardly seemed to notice her presence, as she leant in, over Nigel, continuing to stroke his brow.

Betty went into the WC and searched in what they rather optimistically named 'the medicine cabinet'. It contained little more than a medley of plasters, some old cough syrup and aspirin. Eventually, she came across a dented tin of Germoline. She opened it – the bright pink contents and the distinctive, sharp scent seemed to imply it was still good to use.

When she came back into the sitting room, Nigel had closed his eyes.

"Is he… do you think maybe?" Betty didn't finish her sentence. Hoped Sandra would interpret her concern.

"A doctor, you mean?" she answered.

"Mmmmng!" Nigel gave a disapproving sound to the contrary, through a closed mouth.

"Am-bu-lance?" Betty said, in a stage whisper.

"Mmmmmmmmmmmmng!" Nigel said. He opened his eyes and attempted to lift his head. "No!"

"Sshh, OK darling. No ambulance."

Betty placed the antiseptic cream on the floor, next to Sandra. She watched as her friend gently dabbed at the patches of skin within her reach, with the scrunched tip of the towel, after dipping it in the bowl of water. Gradually, she carefully manoeuvred him to reveal his right leg, unpeeling his trouser leg from his bleeding shin and knee. She shushed his grumbles and coaxed him along. He was docile, awkward, a newborn foal.

The cut on his leg wasn't deep, thank goodness, but the graze extended for at least twelve inches and was punctured with grit and dirt. Betty winced at the sight of Sandra's touch as she dabbed, and wiped, to clean it.

"I'll make some tea," Betty said, after a few minutes, wanting to feel helpful once more.

She found herself moving cautiously and slowly in the kitchen – trying to keep herself occupied for as long as possible, and not wanting to disturb Nigel. She left the kettle boiling on the hob for a while, its whistle removed, steam flowing from the spout into the kitchen in a cloud. After a few more minutes, Sandra appeared through the double doors and pulled them partially closed behind her.

"He's sleeping."

"Is he… Are you sure it's sleep? He's not banged his head? He could be unconscious."

"Not unless that leads to snoring, no. I think he could be plastered, actually. Drunk."

"Really?"

"He certainly smells like it."

Betty nodded, picked up the kettle and filled the teapot. "Has he told you anything?"

Sandra shook her head.

"He's taken a beating though, obviously. Who would do that? You don't think he's been mugged?"

"No, it won't be that," Sandra said, flatly. She went to the fridge and took a fresh bottle of milk from inside the door. Betty watched her, in a daze, as Sandra started to pick at the foil of the bottle, a thick layer of yellow cream still settled around the neck, inside. She had an urge to shake it, to mix it up.

"How do you know?"

"I… well, I just do." She continued to tug at the lid. Betty noted that the nail and tip of her index finger were stained with Nigel's blood.

"But how?"

"Because it's not the first time." She pulled the foil back, and thick, oily milk splashed onto the countertop. Sandra passed the bottle to her and stared her in the eye. "Because he's a homosexual."

*

It was late by the time William returned from taking Nigel home. 10:30pm.

They had been gone for so long that Betty had started to think something had gone awry – Nigel had passed out, or they had run into more trouble. All sorts of scenarios ran through her brain. She was sitting in William's chair, hugging the cushion that they had used to cradle Nigel's head. A small smudge of blood from his lip stained the corner, she noticed. She hugged it tighter still.

Eventually, she heard Sandra and William whispering in the corridor, the gentle creak of the front door as it closed, and then Robert's voice which joined them briefly. The door to the basement flat had been propped open all evening, while he waited for their return. Betty listened as he welcomed Sandra home affectionately and gave effusive thanks to William.

William came into the room and then jumped at the sight of her.

"Why are you sitting in the dark?" he asked. "You made me jump, darling. I assumed you were in bed." He came over to the chair where she sat and bent over, kissing the top of her head. She reached her arms up around his neck and they stayed for a moment in an awkward embrace.

She dropped the cushion. "Shall I make you tea? I've had gallons."

"I think I'd like alcohol," he said. "Beer."

She nodded, and stood, plumping the cushion before she returned it to the chair and indicated for him to sit down. He almost fell into the chair, his long limbs folding up in a concertina. She made her way into the kitchen, turning on a lamp as she did so.

William had returned after work, while the two women were still standing in the kitchen. He had burst into the sitting room singing a song from The Mikado. This was one of his little foibles – to sing light opera, and then quiz her until she named the tune.

He had got as far as "Three little maids from—" when he stopped abruptly and cried "Jesus!" at the sight of the patient. Betty and Sandra had come out to find him in the middle of the room, briefcase dropped to the floor beside him.

"It's Nigel," Betty said, in hushed tones. "Sshh!"

"I can see that. But what the bloody hell happened to the poor bloke?" He stepped forward, tentatively, towards him.

"Isn't it obvious?" Sandra muttered. William glanced up at her.

At that moment, Nigel opened his eyes and put one arm down to his side in a bid to sit up. He winced.

"Steady, old fella, easy there," William said, rushing towards him.

William, calm and steady William, took the helm. He asked no more questions about how or why, and focused instead on assessing Nigel's injuries, only relenting about immediate medical attention when Nigel promised to go to the doctor the next day if he had any ominous symptoms. He reviewed him from top to toe, asking specific questions that the two women had not thought of. Did he lose consciousness at any point? Could he have any internal injuries? Did he have any loose teeth?

"No. No. No… It's not as bad as it looks. Besides, these fine young ladies here have been marvellous nurses," Nigel slurred: his bottom lip was swollen, mouth distorted.

"We have not," Sandra said. "You fell asleep before I could even apply any ointment. Besides, you didn't even know we were there most of the time."

"On the contrary, darling," he said. By now he was upright, and Betty watched as William took his leg and propped it up on the coffee table. "You both showed great kindness to this silly, old fairy."

"Don't say that." Sandra scowled. "You know I hate it when you say that."

"What do you prefer then? Poofter? Shirt lifter?"

"Stop it!" Sandra said.

Nigel started laughing, harshly, a cruel, unnatural sound. His nose was wrinkled, mouth spread wide until he winced at the tension on his scabbing lip.

"Steady on, now. There are women here. I know you've had a shock but still… There's no need to talk like that." William cupped Nigel's shoulder and gave it a gentle tug.

Nigel stopped smiling and looked down at his fingers, now bloody, where he had dabbed at his lips. Within seconds his face contorted again, this time into a grimace. Betty thought he might cry. William gave him a shake again.

"Don't let them get the better of you, old man. Don't let them."

"You know, we should go the police," Betty said. Everyone looked at her. "This is assault. And – and – homosexuality, it's legal now, isn't it? You're over twenty-one. You're not doing anything wrong.

So, you should report this. It's… it's assault. Isn't it?" She looked from one to the other of them, waiting for someone to agree.

"Yes, it is," was all William said.

Sandra nodded.

"You are right, of course, my dear, sweet, Betty. It is battery. And I have not broken the law. And I can't say I even fought back: I'm no fool. The odds were stacked against me. But… sweet child, there are a million reasons why I shan't be reporting it."

"But—" Betty began.

Nigel put his hand up and raised his voice a notch.

"This time, or the next."

Chapter Twenty
Betty (Then)

It wasn't her place to be upset. Not really. She felt almost guilty about how much it had bothered her. It seemed somehow obscene – as if she were trying to make the evening about her – when poor Sandra, and Nigel especially, suffered so much.

But she couldn't stop thinking about it.

And crying.

It had been two weeks and each morning a vision of Nigel curled as a dormouse, bloody lip, appeared shortly after waking. And she knew he was losing patience with it but nonetheless she kept grilling William in the evening. She was both horrified and fascinated by the subject.

Tonight, she had made William an egg salad, and she wondered if it was enough after a hard day at work. She had wanted to cook a pie and had even been to the grocer to pick up some ingredients. But the heat persisted, its heavy, still, warmth stifling and dampening her appetite. After her trip to the shop, she found herself dozing off on the sofa. At the moment, she struggled to eat at all. A salad seemed more appropriate; besides, she had little time for anything else, once she had woken. She didn't tell William about the nap. She was ashamed to be lounging like a lady of leisure.

"So, the law has changed. It is actually in force now. We aren't in some sort of legal limbo while we wait for the act of parliament to be enacted – put into action, somehow?"

"Darling, we've been through this. Yes, it is now legal for consenting men to have a homosexual relationship. Behind closed doors, at least."

She noted he was pushing the last of his lettuce around the plate, mopping up the salad cream. She still had half her meal, untouched, before her. She rose and got him some sliced bread without comment. He took two slices.

"OK, but what I don't understand is why everything has to be so… furtive? On the wireless today, they were talking about people 'comporting themselves with dignity' and not sort of flaunting it. If the law says there is nothing wrong, then how can it be flaunting? What is there to flaunt?"

"I imagine not everyone is comfortable with homosexuality. You can't really expect things to change overnight. It makes some people uneasy. I can't say I am 100%... Look, think of your mother. No – think of my father! How would he feel about Nigel?"

"Yes, but that's wrong, isn't it? I mean, women didn't use to be able to vote but if I went down to the ballot box no one would accuse me of flaunting my rights. Or being undignified."

Nigel laughed.

"I'm serious! And I certainly wouldn't be assaulted for it." Her voice wobbled.

He dropped his fork and reached across the table to her. "You're right, darling. But social mores and legal positions are not always easy bedfellows. You are a funny thing. One minute you've never met a homosexual and the next you're plotting to join some sort of hardcore campaign group. You'll be protesting outside parliament next."

"It's not that," she said. She felt herself on edge, irritated. "I only want to understand. None of it makes sense. It doesn't seem fair."

"No. It doesn't wholly make sense, no. But some things you really just have to accept. Now, are you eating that or am I getting seconds?"

She passed her plate over to him and began to clear the rest of the table, her mind full of images and words, her stomach full of butterflies.

*

The following day, Betty knocked on the door of the basement flat. Sandra had invited her round for tea. They had seen each other the day after Nigel was attacked – but then only in passing a couple of times since. Betty was glad of the invite, as it assuaged her fears that their burgeoning friendship had been fractured by the incident, somehow.

"Come in!" Sandra called out.

Betty made her way down the narrow staircase. The steep drop and the summer warmth left her feeling lightheaded and uncomfortable.

"Long time no see," she said, as she descended. "This blooming heat hasn't gone anywhere yet, has it?"

"Do you find it hot? I'm just starting to notice a difference. It's cooler this week, I thought," Sandra said. She was at the back of the flat in the kitchen space, retrieving cups and plates from the cupboard.

Betty took in the room: cosy but cluttered. There was a large sketchbook on the coffee table with dozens of charcoals and pencils scattered beside it.

Sandra caught her eye. "I've been staying here more. To work, I mean. I'm between commissions and I can't say I'm feeling terribly inspired. So I've been sketching, instead. Some might say doodling."

"How are you?" Betty asked.

"I'm fine. Better get my act together with the artwork or we will start to struggle with the bills."

"Really?" Betty asked, thinking of her mum's warning.

"Don't worry – it's more a case of cutting back on nights out than of shutting off the electric at the moment."

Betty smiled, unsure whether to sit. "Good-o."

"Brother dear has gone across to visit mater for a few days. He left this morning. He won't be telling her what happened, of course, though even to those who choose not to notice such things, I should imagine his shiner was still pretty obvious to her when he arrived. Or at least, the fat lip would be."

"Shiner? He had a black eye, too, then? Blimey. They really did beat the poor soul."

"Yes, quite. Anyway, he dropped this off on the way. I've had it in a tin. Fingers crossed it hasn't collapsed."

Betty moved over to where Sandra stood and watched as she popped open a large metal tin, which had originally housed chocolates. It was upside down, and she slowly lifted it to reveal an intricate construction of crumbly, biscuity cake, layered with cream and sliced strawberries. She could smell it: vanilla, butter and sharp fruit filled the air.

"Oh, my goodness!" she cried. "Did he… did he make that? What is it?"

"He did. He's quite the baker. It's for you; to thank you." Sandra grinned, proudly.

"It looks marvellous!" Betty said, touched. She felt her eyes fill.

"It should taste great, too," Sandra said, with a smile. "It's a Strawberry Shortcake. I'll give you the recipe."

Chapter Twenty-One
Betty (Now)

Paul had been to see David that afternoon, Jonty had assured her. He promised to get David showered and fed and to check on his war wounds.

Betty was tired. She showered early that evening, wondering, not for the first time, if she should consider adapting the bathroom in some way. She had an over-the-bath shower, which meant clambering in and out over the high sides. In January, she had slipped getting out; she still recalled clearly the moment of panic as her left foot skidded on the tiles – rising up into the air before her and moving her lower body into an obtuse angle. She had badly damaged a muscle in her groin and sported a large purple bruise on her inner thigh for weeks. She told no one.

Perhaps a rail would be enough. Maybe young April would do it for her.

The day had rattled her more than she would have liked. She felt oddly responsible for David, she realised, now that Doreen was no longer around. She was something of a mother figure she supposed – no, grandmother, no doubt. If he struggled, she felt it too. And wondered if she could have done more to prevent it. But this was all the more reason to look after her own health. She could not afford to be the next to collapse or fall.

Again, an image of her mother came to mind. She had been so much younger than Betty was herself, now, at the time of her passing. Only sixty-eight.

When the call came, she had been confused at first. They had only had the telephone for a few months, and it had never rung at night. She had heard the ring, and it had enmeshed with her dreams, but it was some time before she had responded. Later, she was told they had rung three times before she had answered. She felt guilty, still, about this. The wait she had given her brother, John. The extra minutes her mother lay on the floor alone, while he went next door to call Betty. It was only when William had prodded her awake that she had realised. Only then that she ran downstairs to take the call.

For some reason, John had called her first. She had never understood why he dialled repeatedly until she answered, not once considering a call to the ambulance service or a doctor. But it was late, and he was young. He had come home from the pub to find her, spreadeagled, on the kitchen floor. And she remained there: unmoving, cold, by the time Betty and William had arrived.

It was a stroke, they said. She could not have been saved.

But the guilt was still there.

*

Betty was watching the television when she first smelled the smoke. For a few minutes, she had been aware of it, without registering its significance. She

112

stood up, knees stiff, and followed the scent. Initially, she thought it was coming from an appliance. She assured herself that if it was serious, her smoke detector would have sounded. And the tenants were very good at helping her to ensure that sort of thing was maintained. If the fire was in one of their homes, she would have heard the sound of an alarm by now.

It didn't take long to realise that the smoke was coming from the garden. It had a thick, woody undertone. Through the small window in the kitchen area, the orange flames flickered and wobbled in the textured glass.

Her heart sank. It would be David.

She walked back over to the sofa and retrieved the slippers she had kicked off, and she made her way outside.

*

Drunk, hysterical, or possibly even drugged: she wasn't sure what to make of his behaviour, but she knew she was out of her depth. He staggered, can of lager in hand, shoes undone. He was far away, on another plane. Her words mingled with the smoke and embers and never quite made their way through to him.

"Now, David, why not come inside with me and have a cup of tea? It's rather late for this type of thing, don't you think? It'll wait until tomorrow. Come, now." She tried to keep her tone light and breezy. She tried.

His voice rose up in a wail at everything she said. Disjointed words and phrases. He didn't even

113

attempt to respond to her words; said whatever came to mind. He cried out that she was gone. He was alone.

It was his fault.

She noted, thankfully, that the fire was dying out. She moved cautiously toward him, stalking. "Oh dear," she said, glancing at the pile of possessions and rubbish he had heaped onto the lawn. "You can't be thinking of throwing all of this without sorting it. I can see a couple of things there you might want. You should do this tomorrow when you have good light and a clear head."

He simply scowled at her. And took another swig.

"David, this… job. You have been working so carefully on it. You can't be thinking of throwing it all?" She was repeating herself, struggling to think of what to say. In truth, he probably should throw it all. But not like this. Not out of spite and guilt.

"Yes, I bloody can. She's not here to stop me, is she? She's not here." He threw something small down onto the top of the pile. A photograph. It floated down, arcing side to side, as a leaf. "I've made up my mind," David cried, bringing both hands to his face.

There was a pause and he began to wail. Betty had lived, long and hard, but she had only heard this sound once or twice in her life. It was guttural. Raw. An indistinct sound beyond words.

Betty moved along the slabs of the garden path. She was almost within touching distance. The fire was out.

"Dear David, that's true. But not tonight. Leave it as it is, and sleep on it. You can decide in the

114

morning. You've had a difficult day and…" She trailed off, wondering if she should have mentioned what had happened.

He did not acknowledge her. He turned on his heel suddenly, wiping his face with his sleeve as he sobbed. He made his way back into the shed.

Then David had a canister of petrol. Betty stopped in her tracks, torn between care for her own safety and fear for his.

One, two… he rammed the matches he retrieved from his pocket against the edge of the packet, and they failed to light – his force and discoordination made it seem unlikely any would.

But then, on his third attempt, a feeble, pale flame popped into existence and cut through the evening light. He dropped it.

There was a swell of flames, a wave. It was instant, huge, bright. Betty staggered back in a reflex, but David seemed transfixed. Absent. Standing less than six feet from the bonfire.

"David!" she cried. He stepped back, and she hoped he would come to her at last, but he simply made his way to the shed.

She heard a noise behind her, and turned, for a moment imagining that the house would be ablaze for some reason – but it was Paul, pushing her back door open with a crack as he rushed towards them. She stared at him, for a moment confused, until he gestured with one thumb up to the window of his flat, above. She saw April there, a shadowy, solitary figure, frowning, leaning close to the glass to take in the scene. She gave a small wave, but April didn't see her.

"Steady on, mate," Paul said, as David came back

out of the shed carrying bin bags: bursting, dusty. Paul lunged towards him, both to help and stop him.

David looked annoyed to see him there and brushed off his words and fingers. Doreen's old brown dress flopped out of the top of the bag; a pale green sheet burst from the side. Betty watched as the sleeve of the dress caught on the latch of the door. David yanked in anger, and it stayed put, a mockery of a woman, stretching out, holding onto the door frame for dear life. Eventually, it ripped, leaving a strip of fabric in its wake, flapping like old bunting.

He dropped the full bin bag of fabric onto the fire. It smouldered and then erupted into flames.

And that was when the shed began to burn.

Chapter Twenty-Two
Betty (Then)

She pulled the potatoes from the rack; certain she had smelt burning. But no, it was only a spot of fat on the base of the oven: not the potatoes themselves. The hot smoke burst forth in a cloud and caught the back of her throat.

This wasn't something she had done many times. Since they'd been married, they'd either been living with William's parents, working through the home improvements or in the midst of this very long, hot summer. Roast dinners had a limited appeal. She'd helped Dorothy often enough, of course, but she had never been wholly convinced that the amount of oil and fat she had used (copious quantities of both) was needed. But Sandra had invited them for Sunday lunch; Betty had insisted on bringing something with them as she still hadn't managed to return the favour of a dinner party.

Her stomach heaved as the heat of the oven combined with the humid warmth of the kitchen, and the smell of lard hit her. She had hardly eaten all weekend, yet the idea of a roast meal on a day like this still did not appeal, in all honesty. But she was keen to see Sandra and Robert. And they hoped Nigel would be joining them, too.

William appeared beside her. He bent down to grab a potato as she started to slip them back into the oven for another ten minutes.

She pushed the tray in quickly and slapped at his fingers with her tea towel.

"It is simply inhumane, the waiting. Who in their right mind eats Sunday lunch at dinner time?" He pulled a face, lips pursed, while simultaneously pretending to reopen the oven door.

"It's hardly dinner time, darling. It's only 3pm." She edged in front of the glass.

"But we probably won't be sat down until four, will we? Mummy always gave me lunch at two."

"Did she? Maybe you would rather eat with Mummy, then." She jabbed him in the chest with her index finger.

"Hhmm. Bright green, sloppy cabbage cooked in bicarb. Burnt parsnips. On second thoughts…" He kissed her cheek. She leant into him.

"I hope my spuds taste OK. It's hardly the most sophisticated of offerings. And I didn't even have any dripping." He stroked her hair.

"They smell fantastic. I'll eat them, even if the others all turn up their nose. I shall sacrifice myself; don't you worry."

"I'm not sure that's particularly reassuring." She laughed.

*

At 3:30, they knocked on the door of the basement. Betty had placed her potatoes into a serving dish: another wedding gift that was making its first appearance. Her mum had been mortified

118

when she saw it: enamel, with a pattern of brown flowers on the side. "You want China," she had said. "And something pretty, like painted roses. Not these ridiculous pictures you get everywhere nowadays, that look as if a four-year-old has done them." Betty had ignored her, and a great-aunt had come up trumps and purchased the pot for her instead.

Sandra opened the door, and they followed her downstairs: Betty holding the pot carefully in front, like a chalice. Sandra smiled up at them, radiant, wearing an orange shift dress, with striped capped sleeves. It was a mini – so short that it was barely a dress at all. Beneath, she had on loose, striped shorts that peeped out, into view, as she moved. Green, orange, white.

"Nice shorts, Sandy," William said. Betty was surprised he had noticed.

"I don't know, man. I prefer this outfit without them," Robert said, wiggling his eyebrows up and down, and holding out his hands as if to grab her.

"Sex pest," Sandra said. William laughed. Betty blushed.

"Ignore her. She's just grumpy because the chicken still isn't ready," said Robert. William nudged Betty, who was momentarily confused.

"Oh, we don't mind waiting, do we darling?" he said and nudged her again. The blush took hold, furiously, as she edged away to stop him from repeating his illicit signals.

"Sit down, anyway. We have cheese straws." Robert pulled a chair out for Betty, but she was still holding the dish.

"I'll just…" she walked over to Sandra, who turned and hugged her, then took the potatoes.

"Sit down. Eat the cheese things. We're still waiting on brother anyway. He's the reason we are eating at this time as he's only coming back from mother's this morning."

Robert, William and Betty all sat together at the table. Betty looked around and noted that they had tidied up. There were no sketchbooks to be seen. She wondered if Sandra was back to painting or had a commission. Robert picked up the open bottle of red wine and made to pour her some. She put her hand over the glass to prevent him.

"Not for me. I suffered too much last time."

He gestured to William, who pushed his glass forward.

"I don't think we've got much else, do we, Sandy?" he called over to her, as she bent over the stove, stirring.

"No, honestly, a soft drink would be great. I have something upstairs if you need me to pop back…"

Sandra kicked the fridge with her foot, still stirring. "Squash," she said. "I put it in there to keep it cold. Don't worry, Betty. This really is just a quiet lunch – no late-night dancing in the offing, this time."

"That's rather a shame," said William.

Just as Robert stood to fetch her a drink, Nigel came in via the backdoor. His lip was no longer swollen, but there remained a crusted, deep red scab. Around his eye, there was the yellow shadow of a bruise. But he was smiling and strode into the room with confidence and ease.

"What are you wearing?" Sandra asked, leaning over to allow him to kiss her cheek. "You look forty."

"Charmed, I'm sure," he replied. He wore a checked jacket with wide lapels, and a pristine, open-necked white shirt. Grey trousers. Black leather shoes.

"No, but you must be boiling. Did you travel in that?"

"Indeed. One must always make an effort." As he spoke, he continued to stride across the room towards the table. He held out his hand to William. "My dear sir," he said. "I am so glad to see you again." He turned to Betty. "Not forgetting my little sis." He leant over her, one arm around the back of her chair as he ruffled her hair and kissed her forehead.

"Hey! You only have one sister and don't you forget it. The bloomin' cheek." Sandra teased.

"Sorry my dear, but that's no longer the case. She is my honorary sister. And nothing that happens from here on in shall ever change that."

Sandra carried a bowl of peas to the table.

"Well, do sit yourself down next to little sis, then. Lunch is served."

*

The meal was wholesome and huge. Betty struggled to eat it all, surreptitiously passing over potatoes and stuffing to William. Sandra repeatedly apologised that they were eating chicken, not beef, but the price of red meat had skyrocketed. No one seemed to mind. Their plates were laden with meat, potatoes, three vegetables and bread sauce.

The others had finished their second bottle of wine as Nigel was relaying the amusing story of the time he attempted to bring a boyfriend to his mother's for lunch. He had been determined to tell her the truth that day but hadn't accounted for the fact that not only was this young man homosexual but vegetarian, no less.

"Truly bohemian! I had warned her, of course. And at the time she seemed to take it in her stride. But then she couldn't understand why he declined a ham omelette to go with his meal – '*but it's not meat, it's an omelette!*'. She thought he was dreadfully fussy and peculiar. The thought of then telling her about his other persuasions. And, in so doing, confirming mine… I didn't want to risk a heart attack at the dining table."

Sandra took a sip of wine and then coughed on it as she laughed, suddenly remembering something. "Oh! Tell them about the potatoes!" She could hardly speak— laughing through her words.

Nigel chuckled and shook his head. "Yes, she was terribly thoughtful. She roasted him a separate batch so he wouldn't have any of the meat juices on them. *That* she had thought of, somehow. Yes, terribly thoughtful. When she roasted them *in water.*"

"In water?" William asked. "I don't… I don't understand. How?"

"Exactly!" said Sandra, slapping the table.

There was a lull, and Betty began tidying the table. Robert took this as a cue to invite the men to pop outside. The two women glanced at one another. No doubt there would be marijuana involved. She wondered if William would indulge. It seemed unlikely. But possible.

Betty continued to pile up the plates as Sandra started to put away the condiments and clear the glasses. Betty scraped the remains of Robert's sauce and peas onto her own leftovers and saw the juices curdle together: the fat of the meat gravy floating on the top of the mess of food, settling in small white specks of fat where it had cooled. She closed her eyes, briefly. When she opened them, Sandra was watching her.

"Are you feeling alright?"

"Oh yes, it's this damn heat," Betty said.

"Right, it's just that you haven't eaten much, and you look a bit peaky." She stood, mid-movement, one hand on the open cupboard door.

"Do I? I have been feeling a bit sort of queasy but I'm fine."

"So, you aren't...?" Sandra didn't finish her sentence but leant forward, her laden hands resting on the table as she lifted one brow.

"I'm not what?" Betty asked.

"You know!"

"No. I... Oh! Goodness me, no. Why would you think that?" She realised with a jolt what she was implying. "In fact, I'm... well, I'm due now and that might be part of it. I've always struggled with my monthlies."

"Right. You're due. And newlywed. And you feel sick. And you're pale. But nooooo. Definitely no chance!"

Betty frowned. She found herself irritated by the conversation. It was intrusive. Insensitive.

"No, there's no chance." She hoped that would be an end to the conversation.

"You're on the pill, then?"

Betty blushed again, but this time in irritation. She turned and put the plates on the side, next to the sink.

"No. I'm not on the pill. But there's no chance because if you must know, there's not a great deal of action in that department. Unlike Robert, William is not a sex pest." She dropped the cutlery into the sink and turned on the hot tap. Sandra came over light on her feet and turned the tap off. She stood close to Betty; then she took her by the shoulders and turned Betty to face her when she didn't acknowledge her.

She kept her hands on Betty's shoulders as she spoke. "I'm sorry." She paused and made eye contact before she continued. "Nosey cow-itis again. You should tell me to bloody shut up. I wouldn't be offended."

"Bloody shut up," Betty said.

They hugged. Sandra slid her hands down the other woman's arms until her fingers touched hers, and they stood hand-in-hand together.

"You can talk about it if you want to. Or not."

"Thank you. But there's not much to say. We have… you know… consummated things. But we aren't… we don't… And to be honest, I'm not really sure why. I keep hoping things will click into place."

"I see. Well, we're all different. There's time." said Sandra. She looked to the floor. "But if you have… then there is a small chance, right? It's not impossible."

"Bloody shut up!" Betty cried, pretending to slap her arm. They both laughed, though Betty felt the prick of tears, forming. "Yes, right. OK. A very small chance, I suppose."

"Told you," Sandra said, winking as she turned back to finish clearing the table.

*

They stayed downstairs until almost 9 pm, though this time they progressed onto tea and coffee rather than beer or more wine. Nigel sat between Betty and William on the sofa and told more stories about his visits home: his mother's bemusement at his neckerchief-wearing-ways and her horror at Sandra's unbecoming behaviour. But there was a lot of affection there, she noted. He grinned broadly when he spoke of her, which he did a lot. She wondered if he struggled with the fact, that he couldn't share everything about his life with his mother. Unlike Sandra, who seemed to want to pull ever further away.

It had been a comfortable, informal afternoon. Robert was on the floor, barefoot, heavy-eyed. Sandra sat in the chair behind him and fiddled with his hair, occasionally. It struck Betty that Sandra and Robert were the first couple that they had ever spent so much time with, and she was delighted to find that it felt so easy. They really were friends, now. Good friends. And William seemed to enjoy spending time with them. With Nigel, too.

When they finally climbed the stairs back inside, Betty continued up to the next floor, not stopping downstairs. She was surprised to find that William followed her.

"I'm having an early night," she said, over her shoulder. "I've been feeling hot and bothered all day."

He nodded. "But you don't have to come with me. I know you like to sit up. I'm just being an old lady."

"I don't mind," he answered. "I have work tomorrow and it's been a long day. Besides, I rather like the idea of being next to you."

She continued to make her way to the bedroom, and he followed, not even stopping at the bathroom as they passed it. She went into the room and closed the curtains, save a small gap. It wasn't quite dark yet. She had left the window wide open. The smell of the summer evening permeated the room.

The room was tidy and the furniture new, but the wallpaper remained the same since the day they had moved in. In the corner on her side, the paper had lifted and was beginning to peel away where it joined. This would be her next project. This would give her something to do. Not that she had ever wallpapered before.

She sat on the edge of the bed and unbuttoned her blouse; yawning as she slipped off her watch and rings and placed them on the bedstand. She stood, to remove her cigarette pants and top, and realised William was watching her. He came over to her, slipping the sheer fabric over her shoulder, kissing her clavicle as the blouse fell down. He did the same to the other side until it hung behind her from her arms – her underwear, chest, and stomach exposed and pale in the evening light. She allowed it to fall to the floor. He leant in and kissed her breastbone, then up her throat towards her face and she smelt him: his usual scent mixed with sweet, dull smoke, red wine and coffee. She kissed him back, but then pulled away, suddenly. She had to. The smell and the heat were too much. This was overwhelming, unexpected. Strange.

"Darling, I… I really don't feel that great," she said. He stayed close to her face and then kissed her gently on the forehead before bending down to retrieve her blouse.

"Then we'd best get you to bed," he said, kindly.

Chapter Twenty-Three
Betty (Now)

Betty sat, drinking elderflower cordial in the late afternoon sun, listening to April talk. She felt comfortable with this young woman: there was a strange familiarity there. She was forthright, of course, but she found that April would listen and reflect during a conversation. She was the sort of person who might actually say: 'I see. I've changed my mind. I was wrong.' This was a rare quality, these days. Something to be cherished.

They had been there for at least thirty minutes already. They flitted between comfortable silence and easy conversation.

Neither one had mentioned the fire.

April was talking about her return to work. She was a primary school teacher, and it seemed that she was obligated to lose much of the last week of her holidays in order to make an effective start to the year.

"Oh, it's better to be ahead of the game. It is worth it, in the long run. I'll clear my emails, finish sorting the first week's lessons, photocopying, getting resources ready, tidying, get to know the profile of my class."

April loved her job and the school she worked at, but was looking for a new challenge, she said. This was hardly a surprise. Jonty had disclosed to

Betty that April had been in an established relationship until recently. Breaking up with a boyfriend; finding a new home. The next step was a job change and a new haircut.

"Why not?" Betty said. "You must do these things while you are still young."

She thought of her time at Bloomer's Bakeries. How young she was. It was a whole lifetime ago. Perhaps she should have stayed there for longer – carried on working after they wed. Maybe things would have been different. Who knows?

April spoke again and Betty noted a tightness, a rising inflection. "Do you know, I thought Paul was some sort of office worker or accountant when I met him."

"Really? You surprise me. Why?" Dear Paul, her kind and steady tenant from number two. He was sensible, yes, in his way. But he had a depth, a sensitivity. Not that accountants couldn't be sensitive. But he was the sort of person who needed a vocation, not a job.

April started to move on, to discuss David, but Betty couldn't bear to think of him. The previous night had been exhausting for them all and she still felt a heavy guilt at the way things had developed. She should have done more. She should have realised exactly how bad things had become.

Besides, she was also keen to work something out. She was biding her time, but she would move the chatter back to Paul, when she could. She had a nagging feeling, from the way April had spoken. Something about her voice, her posture, told her that there might be something there. She was nervous, awkward when mentioning his name. There was something between her and Paul.

Something Betty was more than happy to encourage.

Chapter Twenty-Four
Betty (Then)

It was Thursday, 10 am. For once, the sky was overcast. She had no major plans, and she had slept in. She could not blame overindulgence, rushing, lack of sleep, or the heat. None of these things applied.

But she had thrown up, two mornings in a row.

Betty sat on the edge of the bed, wondering if she was safe to dress and go downstairs, or whether another wave of nausea would be visiting soon. She desperately wanted tea, but William was at work, and she couldn't face the idea of going downstairs to get some.

Perhaps it was glandular fever. Or influenza. But she didn't have a fever, she didn't think.

She wasn't that ill. She mustn't wallow. When she was seven or eight, she had measles. She still remembered vividly the hallucinations she had experienced: so real they had seemed. They were seared into her memory alongside real events. At one stage, she had pictured a giant tarantula climbing up her belly, slowly, the thick hair on its legs spiked as needles. She had finally snapped out of the dream to find her mother beside her, crying her name, her hands encompassing Betty's as she tried to bring her back into the room.

This was nothing like that. So why did she feel so truly pathetic? So sorry for herself? Emotional, even?

She would have liked to see her mother now, she realised, with a jolt. She would have brought her tea and toast and tucked her back into bed. Brusquely, of course.

Tearfully, she allowed herself to flop back down on her side and attempt to get a little more sleep.

*

It was one o'clock before she got out of bed. She washed her hands and face, brushed her hair, and put on a clean nightie. This one was old and full length. The fabric was bobbled and thick, but she found comfort in it. She pulled on a pair of thick socks and made her way downstairs.

As she descended the stairs to the ground floor, Sandra was coming out of the basement flat. For a moment, Betty considered turning on her heel and going back upstairs – she did not want to be seen like this – but it was too late. Sandra glanced up, sensing her or hearing the dull thud of her steps, perhaps. She jumped.

"Goodness. I thought I'd seen a ghost," she said.

"That'll be this rather fetching nightdress," Betty answered. She stood still, halfway down the stairs, unsure what to do.

"Yes, but your face is the same shade as well. Not to be rude. Sorry. I mean… I… are you alright?" Sandra moved closer, coming towards the bottom of the stairs. She had a large black camera hanging around her neck, her left hand instinctively moving to cradle it as she walked.

Betty nodded at it. "Going somewhere interesting?"

"Nothing… But seriously. You don't look well. Has something happened?"

"No. Nothing except a bit of a tummy bug. I feel rotten but it's not serious."

She started to descend the stairs towards Sandra. She felt rather like a naughty child, sneaking downstairs when they should be in bed. There she was, in her ridiculous, unfashionable nightie, hair in a low pony and apparently ghoulish features, walking towards this stylish young woman, her features illuminated in a soft glow by the light through the textured glass of the front door.

"Right," Sandra said, decisively. "I'm staying here with you and playing nursemaid. Have you managed to eat anything? Have you drunk anything?"

"This is the first time I have made it downstairs all day, actually. So, no. Nothing."

"Follow me," Sandra said, opening the door to the sitting room. "I shall be your Florence Nightingale."

*

Betty finished her boiled eggs and most of her toast, plus two cups of tea.

"I can't remember the last time I had soft-boiled eggs," she said. "But they were perfect." She leant back in her chair, glad that she had allowed Sandra to convince her to try something.

Sandra came to sit at the table with her. "Not queasy anymore, then?"

"It comes and goes. But I'm OK right now. Thank you for being so kind."

"Look, I know you might not like me asking but did you start your… are you bleeding yet?"

"You really don't beat about the bush, do you? I don't think I've ever discussed my monthly cycle with anyone as much as you before." It was meant as a joke, but somehow Betty sounded snippy. Her voice was clipped and formal.

Sandra smiled. "What, all of two occasions? You should spend time with my friend Franky. She went into graphic detail about hers on a weekly basis when she and her husband were trying."

"Sorry, I don't mean it really. Though it is true that it's not something I'm particularly used to discussing."

"So does that mean you aren't planning to answer my question?" Sandra teased, leaning forward towards her.

She sighed. "No, it hasn't come. But there has been the odd occasion when I've not been regular. And I've been feeling sick a lot of the time, not just in the morning. And with things the way they are… I just don't think it's that." Betty paused. When she spoke again, her voice was quieter. "In all honesty, I haven't dared to allow myself to get my hopes up."

"I understand that. But you might need to face it. Franky was sick for months with hers, and often right up to the evening. I think it's an old wives' tale to call it 'morning sickness'. Apparently, it doesn't know how to tell the time."

"Really? I had no idea."

"So. How many days late are you?"

"Honestly – I don't actually know," Betty replied.

"Well, we'd better work it out."

*

They spent the next hour or so trying to calculate with precision how overdue she was; Sandra prompted her, by quizzing her, using the news, things that had happened in the house, what she was wearing on specific days – anything to help pin down the date she had last bled. Betty felt ridiculous, not knowing, but it was something that she had never had to consider before. Each month, she was hit by fierce lower back pain, which gave a clear warning that it would be with her within the next twelve hours.

Eventually, with a jolt, she realised that it had been before Sandra and Robert had even moved in. This cycle was on day 32 or 33. She was five days late.

"OK," Sandra said. "And it is possible – within the last month, I mean. You have… you know."

Betty smiled weakly at Sandra. She thought back to the night they had made love. The one and only night. After the dinner party. And how it seemed he had been keen to do so once more, just last Sunday. Again, after they had spent time with Sandra and Robert. What did that mean? Was it a coincidence, or the cause? She shook the thought away.

"Yes. About two and a half weeks ago. No, nearly three."

135

"Well, that would be mid-cycle, which is the danger zone. So that makes sense. Though a little early for you to be having morning sickness, in that case, I think."

"I thought you said it couldn't tell the time?"

"Very true. I should think it's perfectly possible." Sandra reached across the table and grabbed her hands. "Betty Williams, I think you're going to have a baby."

Chapter Twenty-Five
Betty (Then)

She decided not to tell William until she had seen the doctor. Despite Sandra's confidence, it still seemed unlikely that the solitary night of passion had led to pregnancy. The whole experience was surreal, intangible. Without having been trying for a baby, or sporting a baby bump, it felt as if she were pretending, somehow. So, she decided to visit the doctor on the following Monday if she still had the same troubling sickness and no bleeding. The one blessing of their lack of love life was the fact that William was oblivious to her cycles and unlikely to notice anything amiss.

That Sunday, she invited her mum around, along with her brother, John. They had been in the house for months and he still hadn't visited, though she hadn't pressed him to come. They got along in their own way but were not what you might describe as close. But she was still feeling delicate, and a touch nostalgic. It would be lovely to see him and feed them both.

They were coming for a light tea, as Dorothy was entertaining one of her neighbours for lunch. This meant Betty was off the hook regarding cooking a roast and it gave her much of the afternoon to prep. She made a buffet of sorts for them all to choose from: homemade sausage rolls, cold meats, boiled eggs, and tinned vegetable salad.

William went to collect them while she assembled a cheese and pineapple hedgehog, from half a grapefruit and some tin foil. She had considered making some little curried pies that Sandra had told her about, but she doubted mother would be enthralled. This was a safer bet.

By the time he returned, she had placed all of the food on the table, plumped the cushions, and tidied away her magazines. She heard William's usual chatter as he came through the front door, with a few grunts and grumbles from her mother. They came into the room. John was not with them.

"Where's the prodigal son?" she asked.

"Don't ask," Dorothy said, tersely.

William walked towards her, swiftly. "Really, don't ask," he muttered as he went past. "I'll get you that drink I told you about, Dorothy. It'll really quench your thirst."

"Oh yes," Dorothy said, rolling her eyes to Betty once she was out of his line of sight. "Great."

He came back through the double doors clutching a small bottle. "Technically, it is a type of beer, but you drink it chilled and it's very light."

"Go on then, stop bloody talking about it and get it open," Dorothy said.

Betty moved towards her mother and gestured to take her coat. "Sit down, Mum. I'll bring you a snack. Go at this end of the sofa and I can put it on the side table."

"Couldn't afford more than one table, I suppose?" Betty didn't respond but made her way into the kitchen where William was popping open three bottles of lager.

"What on earth…?" she whispered to him, in a hiss.

"John. He's gone and *knocked someone up*."

"What? I don't believe it. Are you sure?"

"According to your mother, yes. She certainly seems pretty definite about it."

From the other room, Dorothy called out to them. "What's all that whispering about? I may be old, but I'm not deaf, yet. Or stupid. Come back in here and you can hear it all from the horse's mouth." Betty and William looked at one another.

"Come on, then," William said. "Let's see what the old filly has to say."

*

In the end, it was the only topic of conversation for the whole evening.

She was just seventeen, the young woman in question, so six years his junior. They'd only been dating for a couple of months. He had proudly announced their engagement at the dinner table that same day, Dorothy said.

"There's me with a mouth full of Yorkshire and he stands up and tells the world he'll be getting married next month. I could have swung for him. I've got Mrs Jones and her sister – visiting from Wales, she is – well, they're congratulating me on one side and your bloody brother is grinning like a daft ape on the other."

"And what about the girl? Tell me about her? I don't even know her name," Betty said.

They were sitting at the table, with plates of food surrounding them. Betty had placed some on her plate, but she found herself pushing it around with a fork. She wasn't sure if it was due to the news, or nausea. William was silent, slowly making his way through a generous portion of ham.

"Oh, *her*. Linda, her name is. Linda Stroodle-doodle: something foreign-sounding her surname is. Lord knows where her parents are from."

"Mother!" Betty scolded.

"It's true! Anyway, she's a pretty little thing but hardly brain of Britain. She wouldn't have made it into your fancy school, I can tell you that. She works in the factory, and she's always caked in makeup. Great thick lines on her eyelids. More interested in her looks than anything else. Not like you."

"Um… Is that a compliment or are you saying I don't take care of myself?" Betty was amused.

"Both," she answered. "Anyway, I can't stand the girl. You have to ask her fifteen direct questions before you get so much as a one-word answer. Spends her life giggling and shrugging at everything, looking over to our John to answer for her. No backbone."

"Also unlike Betty," William said, quietly.

"Quite," Dorothy said.

Betty pretended to slap him on the arm. "I'm sure she's just nervous, Mum. I mean, you can be a little intimidating."

"I am not! Anyway, then he waits until after lunch to drop into conversation that she's having a baby. I mean, I worked that part out myself but didn't want to be airing our dirty washing in front of Mrs Jones, so I'd said nothing… but I mean —

married in three months? Planning a wedding in four weeks? You don't have to be Sherlock Holmes to figure that one out."

"Anyway, however, it's happened. It's done now. And really, it's good news, isn't it? A bit… sudden, I grant you, but I remember you were worried at one stage that you'd never be rid of him. It will be good for him to get married and move on. He'll grow up."

Dorothy reached over the table and took the platter of chicken, tipping much of it onto her own plate. Betty felt her stomach lurch as it fell onto the pickle and salad cream.

"You haven't heard the best part, though, have you? He's not moving on. He thinks he's bloody living with me. The three of us and their brat, all under my roof. Well, he can think again."

*

After they'd finished eating, they moved back to the sitting room. Betty was glad to be able to sit comfortably again and allowed her mother to ramble on about all the ways in which John had let the family down. He had no savings, it transpired, even though he earnt almost £800 a year and paid little in the way of rent. It was unclear where his wages went but Dorothy speculated that he liked to throw his money around when he went out and that this was the reason he had attracted Linda.

"I should hope there's more to it than that. But I thought you wanted to be a grandmother, Mum," Betty said. "You've certainly given me that impression."

141

"I want to be a grandmother. I don't want to be an unpaid nursemaid for a young couple without two pennies to rub together."

"Fair enough," William said. Betty looked over to him, surprised. "Well, your mother does have a point, dear. Babies are a lot of work." He wrinkled his nose and looked down into his glass. "Messy. Noisy. I can't say I'm their biggest fan – and the last thing Dorothy needs at her time in life is to be taking on that kind of responsibility and upset."

"Exactly," Dorothy said.

"Messy and noisy? Upset? That's rather a narrow view, don't you think?"

"On the contrary," he said, voice flat. "I should say it's a realistic one."

Chapter Twenty-Six
Betty (Then)

The weekend had been and gone. Nothing had changed. It was time to bite the bullet.

Betty managed to get up and ready by 10:30 am; ironically, by the time she had finished tea and toast, she didn't feel queasy at all. But she knew that this was not enough to justify avoiding the doctor. Only the night before, she had been unable to eat. Besides, her monthly still had not come.

Nine days late.

The surgery was across the other side of the park – easily within walking distance. She put on shoes, picked up her bag and went out the front door. She found herself walking a touch faster than was comfortable but couldn't stop. She leant forward, putting weight on the balls of her feet, ignoring the discomfort as her shoes rubbed against her hot skin. Now that she had decided to do this, she wanted it over with.

Usually, she loved to visit this park. She had been delighted when she realised how close it was to Hummingbird House when the property came on the market. It was one of its selling points. She had admired the park for years. She had marked each spring by the bloom of the daffodils; she loved to see the imaginative displays the parkkeeper made each summer with bedding plants: they would sculpt messages; flags; patterns from petunias and pansies. She had spent several afternoons sunbathing on the grass, before they had a home of their own, dozing on a blanket while William read beside her.

But today, the park was busy: there were people exercising dogs; there was a young couple walking arm in arm. Parents. Children. Babies. Everywhere there were people; there was noise. The grit from the path caught the back of her throat and the heat of the sun raised a prickle of sweat on her brow.

Finally, she was out on the other side, where she found herself on the edge of tears – what on earth was the matter with her these days? She stopped and paused. Took three deep breaths. Then crossed the road to the surgery.

*

"Doctor Davies is on his summer holidays, I'm afraid, Miss."

"Mrs.," she corrected.

"Sorry. So, you're Mrs…?"

"Yes," Betty said.

"No, I mean, you are Mrs *Who*?" the receptionist clarified. She looked at her askance, as if unsure if she were unwell or simply stupid.

"Right-o. Sorry. Mrs Betty Williams."

"OK, Mrs Williams. Doctor Davies shan't be back for another two weeks, I'm afraid, but I do have a cancellation for Doctor Janus if you wanted to see someone today."

"Today? I don't know. But two weeks? That's a long time. I… Doctor *Who* did you say?" She knew she was rambling. In all the scenarios that had played out in her mind, she hadn't accounted for this.

"Janus. A cancellation. This morning. In just… fifteen minutes or so, actually." The receptionist enunciated it carefully and was writing her name down into the book as she spoke, clearly assuming a decision had been made.

And so it was: Betty was going to see Doctor Janus.

*

In the end, the wait was closer to thirty-five minutes. Betty sat in the waiting room on a creaky chair and bit her nails – a habit she had thought long broken. By the time her appointment came, the skin around her left thumbnail was raw and pink.

"Mrs Williams?" a voice called into the room. Betty looked up to find a young woman, dressed in a sensible navy skirt, grey blouse, and a white lab coat.

"Yes?" Betty said, confused.

"Doctor Janus," she answered, with a smile. "Come with me."

Betty stood up and found her legs felt disconnected and heavy. Doctor Janus didn't appear to notice; she stayed at the open door of the waiting room, a placid smile on her face, waiting patiently for Betty as she lumbered over. Just as she was about to reach her, Doctor Janus turned and walked towards a small room to the right, at the front of the building. Betty followed.

She'd never been in this room before: it was bright and welcoming, with a pot plant by the window and a small blanket across the back of the patient's chair. But it was surprisingly small. Far smaller than Doctor Davies' room.

"I don't believe we've met before. I've been at the practice for about five months now: I came down from Reading. I must say, I prefer it here. Anyway, take a seat, Mrs Williams, and tell me what is troubling you." Doctor Janus sat back in her chair, gently touching the tips of her fingers together in a peak.

"Call me Betty. I usually see Doctor Davies," Betty said. She had no idea how to launch into the matter.

"Yes, I can see from your notes. He won't be back for a little while. So why don't you tell me, and I'll see how I can help."

"I'm not really sure where to start," Betty said.

"Please," she reassured her. "Take your time."

Betty wondered how young this woman was. Not much older than her, she suspected. Her hair was pushed back in a simple hairband, and she had no makeup on, as far as Betty could see. She had few wrinkles, bar one tight pinch between her brows, and a young complexion: a natural puff of pink to each cheek and an enviably smooth forehead. But there were also some flecks of grey around her hairline, amongst the dark brown hair. And she had a confidence of tone that suggested she was not new at this. She had been here before.

146

"Well." She took a breath. "My menstrual period is very late, and I wondered if I might be… be pregnant." Saying the word was peculiar. Bold and harsh.

"I see. How late, exactly?"

"Nine or ten days, I think."

"And you're usually regular?"

"Not exactly, but I've never been this overdue. Early, if anything." This was true.

"Any spotting? Pain? Any other symptoms?" Her voice was low, words spoken quickly, softly, matter-of-fact.

"No. Oh, but yes. I've been feeling sick a lot. A few times, I've thrown up." The doctor tapped her pen on the desk as she listened and raised her eyebrows at this final comment.

"And you've had marital relations in the last couple of months?"

"Yes, but… well, yes."

"Would you mind if I examined you?"

"Do you want to?" Betty asked, confused.

Doctor Janus chuckled. "It would be helpful. But it's not compulsory."

"I… then, yes." Betty stood and moved towards the bed behind her. She started to unbutton her blouse automatically, and then paused as the Doctor went over to the door and flicked the lock, and started to pull a curtain around the bed.

"Oh!" she said. She didn't recall Doctor Davies ever locking the door.

"It's just for privacy," she said. "Nothing ominous, I promise."

"Sorry, I'm just a bit jumpy," Betty said.

"That's not surprising. If you could slip your top off and lie down on the bed. Now, when you're ready, call me through. You can leave your knickers on and just loosen your trousers, as long as you can slip them down slightly. I'm going to want to feel your tummy."

She did as asked.

She lay still and stared at the ceiling as the doctor prodded her belly; it was uncomfortable but not painful; more humiliating than anything else. She decided to count the ceiling tiles above her. Anything that meant she didn't have to think about the here and now.

"Could you… what about your breasts? Are they swollen at all? Some women find that they have sensitive nipples in the early stages of pregnancy."

"I haven't noticed anything."

"Why don't you check yourself while I slip around to the other side of the curtain again, and make some notes," Doctor Janus said.

"But what am I looking for?" Betty asked, confused.

"Tingling or increased sensitivity."

"Don't you want to check?" She had not known any other doctors to defer to her like this.

"Well, no," Doctor Janus answered, gently. "It's your body, Mrs Williams. You are the best judge of how it usually is, and how it should be."

Doctor Janus slipped through the curtain and pulled the gap shut behind her. Betty felt peculiar, self-conscious as she slipped the straps of her bra down over her shoulders and did as the doctor had asked.

*

She was surprised to note the beginning of blisters on her feet as she started to put on her shoes. She had carried them through to the chair at Doctor Janus' desk to put them back on, and now wished she had attempted this ungainly move behind the privacy of the curtain. She sensed the doctor watching her as she winced and forced her foot in.

"Any sensitivity?" Doctor Janus asked.

For a moment Betty thought she was referring to her feet but then realised, with a jolt, that she meant the examination she'd just performed on herself.

"Yes, actually," she answered. She felt foolish not to have noted this earlier.

Doctor Janus looked down at the card of notes before her, then picked up her pen and added a few more words. She picked it up, held it by the corner and shook it, absently, as one might do wet ink. She paused.

"So, Mrs Williams. It is very likely that you're in the first trimester of pregnancy. Everything seems fine, though it's early days, of course."

"Are you sure?" Betty asked. So, that was it.

"As sure as I can be. Tender breasts, amenorrhea, nausea — all classic symptoms. Is the heat bothering you?"

She looked down to her feet, puffy and red, crammed into her shoes. "A little."

"Your core body temperature rises during pregnancy. It's a normal – though uncomfortable –

symptom. You may also find you are more fatigued."

Betty nodded.

"I'll make a referral for a follow-up. In the meantime, I want you to keep out of the heat, eat as well as you can, and keep a stash of ginger biscuits to hand for that sickness."

Betty nodded again.

"Your husband will be delighted, I assume? And he'll look after you?" Doctor Janus looked directly at her, unblinking. She reminded her of Sandra, for a moment.

"Yes, of course. William is very attentive."

She frowned, slightly. "Good. Perhaps see if he will accompany you to your appointment. It can be helpful for you both to have the information."

Betty couldn't imagine William coming to a maternity appointment. "Right," she said.

"Mrs Williams – Betty – I know it's a lot to take in right now. But you are young enough and healthy. I'm hopeful things will all work out just fine. Come back to see me if you have any concerns or if things… change."

"Thank you, Doctor. I will," she said, as she got up to make her way back to Hummingbird House.

"May I be the first to wish you 'congratulations'," Doctor Janus said, smiling broadly.

Chapter Twenty-Seven
Betty (Then)

"So, she confirmed it, then. You are pregnant."

"Yes, she said it was early days, but with all my symptoms..."

They were sitting at Betty's dining table. Sandra had pulled her chair around, and sat at the corner, one hand resting on the back of Betty's chair. The two women leant forward together, sitting so close that their hair was touching.

*

Betty had returned to the house by one o'clock and ran across the sitting room to rest in William's chair. She pulled off her shoes and threw them across the floor, then curled herself into position: feet up on the seat, arms wrapped around a cushion. She had stayed there, in silence, alone, for at least an hour – perhaps more.

After some time, there was a knock on the sitting room door. She didn't move.

"Hello?" Sandra said, simultaneously opening the door a crack. The door blocked each other's view, but Betty would know her voice anywhere.

Betty didn't want her there; didn't want her to go. She froze, fingers gripping one sore foot, mouth buried into the cushion.

"Hello?" Sandra called again, louder. She didn't open it any further. Betty watched as the door began to close.

"Come in," she said. Her voice was raspy and hesitant. She cleared her throat. "Come in."

"Oh!" the door flung open, and Sandra appeared. "I didn't think you were home." She paused, midway into the room. "Not feeling good, again?"

"No, I'm OK. Just…" She drifted off, unsure what to say, and Sandra rushed to her.

"What's happened?" Sandra had reached her and squatted down in front of the chair. "Tell me."

"I went to the doctor," she whispered.

*

Now they were sat together, drinking the tea that Sandra had made. Betty had told her about Doctor Davies being away. The wait. The woman Doctor. The conversation. Examination. The outcome.

She didn't mention the breast exam.

Sandra sat, unusually quiet, while Betty spoke, taking in all that she had said. Periodically, she had leant in and touched her arm or hand.

"Right. And it's a shock, I suppose. After wanting it, and the pressure from your mother, and the lack of… well, you weren't expecting it." Sandra moved her hand from the back of the chair to rub Betty's neck. She felt both comforted and irritated. She was painfully aware of the sensation. Distracting. Too much.

"Yes. I didn't really imagine it could be true."

152

They sat in silence for a moment. Sandra continued to stroke her neck, periodically, until Betty grabbed her hand and shook her head, swiftly. Sandra simply nodded and stopped.

They lifted their cups, in unison, and drank their tea. It seemed like a comfortable silence, but Betty knew the truth. She knew that Sandra assumed she needed time to digest the news. She expected Betty to assimilate the information and then shift out of this state of mind. To be an ecstatic, glowing mother-to-be. But how could she?

After a while, Sandra made to stand. "More tea?"

"No, I've had plenty."

"Do you mind…?" Sandra asked, gesturing towards the kitchen.

"Help yourself."

She watched Sandra go through the double doors, leaving one ajar. She could hear her moving about the space on the other side: seeing a glimpse of her periodically as she moved from stovetop to sink and back, took the milk from the fridge, and searched for a spoon.

"Have you eaten?" she called. "I could make toast. Or a sandwich?"

Betty didn't answer. Alone again, even if only for a brief moment, she felt herself disintegrate. Copious, forceful tears teemed down, and she was winded, hollow. She bent over. For a moment she cried silently, quickly, in hiccupping sobs – until she ran out of breath. Inhaling deeply, she let out a harsh sound, followed by a deep, hollow, bawl. She shocked herself at the volume but could not control it.

Sandra ran through the doors, a look of panic on her face.

"What on earth…?"

"William," was all she could say, between sobs. "William."

Sandra sat back down next to her, moving into place cautiously. "I think you need to start from the beginning, again. And this time, tell me everything"

Betty told her. She told her how he was so affectionate. Tactile. Considerate. But how he turned away each night in bed. How he rarely looked at her when she undressed. And they didn't mention it, this elephant in the room. This absence.

And then one night, it had happened. It had been unexpected, urgent, loving and tender, and all that she had wanted, but a one-off.

And Betty told her how she had tried not to think of the possibility of pregnancy because surely, she could not hope for it on the basis of one tryst. One solitary night. So, she had not dared to dream or hope. Until last night, she had discovered her baby brother had beaten her to it – his girlfriend, a woman Sandra had never met, was pregnant, which was terrible timing because now her special time was shared and diminished. And her mother was not even excited. So, she suspected – no, she knew – that her own news would simply be a burden now. An extra. A tag-along. Not a special, joyous, precious thing.

But worse than that, worst of all, William had said he did not like children. Outright, he had said it. 'Messy and noisy' he had described them as. The one and only time he had commented on babies –

during the one and only time she was likely to be pregnant – and this is what he said.

He would not be happy with this news. And her mother would not be happy with this news. So how could she be?

"That… that's a lot to take in," Sandra said, after a brief pause. She got up and went to the kitchen, coming back with a piece of kitchen paper that she proffered as a hanky to her.

"Let me see if I've grasped this. Your brother has knocked up a girl. Your mother has given him a piece of her mind. William doesn't like to do the deed and he thinks babies are noisy and messy. Correct? That's the gist?"

"In a crude form, I guess." Betty attempted a laugh but failed. She wiped her face with the clean side of the tissue then crumpled it up and balled it tight, in her hand.

"Ok, well. One: your brother having a baby doesn't take anything away from you. If anything, it's helpful. You can share things and help one another. Two: your mother is bound to be peeved. If he's gone off getting his kicks with some piece of skirt she doesn't know, and now they are doing the whole matrimonial thing backwards, well that's hardly going to put her in the best frame of mind. Plus, it'll cost a pretty penny. But you are a whole other kettle of fish. You're sensible and you aren't dependent on her. She's not going to respond the same way to you."

"Do you think?" Betty asked.

"I know. And finally, old Mr William Williams. Who knows why he likes to look-and-not-touch but at least he is a kind and loyal husband, right? And

155

honestly, if there is a man on Earth who doesn't think babies are messy and noisy then I haven't met him yet." She leant over and put one hand on her arm, tugging it reassuringly. "And he's right, isn't he? Just that men are allowed to say these things and us women aren't."

"I don't know. I mean, we've never spoken about children and to hear those words – those as his first words on the subject – they shocked me. And he wasn't joking. Far from it."

"Oh, they say all sorts of things. You should hear the nonsense that comes out of Robert's mouth sometimes, especially after he's been smoking."

"But that's just it." Betty picked up the ball of tissue again and looked down at the table as she started to rip it into tiny pieces. Snowflakes against the dark wood. "William doesn't talk nonsense." She pulled a tuft, and watched it fall on the tabletop. "And he doesn't smoke." She dropped another. "He's very careful with his words and he's thoughtful. I really think he'll be mortified when he finds out we're having a baby." She sprinkled the rest of the tissue into the air, watching it cascade, and fall in a mess of sodden paper.

Sandra didn't answer her, so Betty looked up, to check her response, but she was looking away, across the room towards the front window. Her eyes were wide, and her lips a touch apart. Betty followed her line of sight, confused.

And there, standing next to the open door, was William.

Chapter Twenty-Eight
Betty (Now)

Between Betty and Jonty, they had managed to engineer a barbecue for the coming Saturday. Jonty had 'spontaneously' suggested it to Betty and April, when he had come across them together sitting outside the front of the house. Although it was about time this happened anyway, especially with all that had befallen the tenants of late.

Betty had then planted an idea in April's head to encourage David to get his hair cut and to clean up. She had turned to her after Jonty had pinned down a date for the occasion and mentioned how he would benefit from encouragement to tidy up his appearance.

"Oh, don't worry. I'll take him. He's not keen on saying no, I've noticed. And I can be quite persuasive."

"Marvellous. What a fantastic idea. And you, my dear? You should treat yourself, at the same time."

April lifted a hand and ran her fingers through her hair. "I suppose it is about time that I had my bi-annual cut. I'm forever putting it off. It's not really a priority for me."

"I can understand that. But one does feel better afterwards, don't you agree? It is usually worth it." She didn't think April needed to do anything to her appearance – she liked how comfortable the young

157

woman looked in her skin – but she also knew the potential power of investing in yourself, as a psychological boost. The same was true of David, to a lesser extent. The long hair was fine, and she could cope with the stubble – but she also knew that self-neglect could reflect self-esteem, and sharpening up might be a small step towards boosting that, too.

"I guess?" April didn't sound convinced.

"A good time of year for you, what with returning to work so soon. You'll be too busy again, soon. I've had a thought…" Betty said. "Why not see if you can both get appointments for Saturday afternoon, before the barbecue? It's a good excuse to have David fresh-shaven and trimmed if he's going to be amongst the whole group of us. And yourself. Always nice to have an event to show these things off. Everyone will be there: Ben, myself, Paul…"

"Right. I see. I guess that makes sense, then. I'll try to arrange that for Saturday. Then we shall both grace you all with our new looks."

"You are clever, dear," Betty said.

*

It was Friday. Jonty and Paul had ensured that the barbecue became what they called a 'working party' where people would be dismantling what remained of the shed and its (saturated and scorched) contents. They had been around to the other tenants, one by one, coaxing them into attending and guilting them into wanting to lend a hand. Ninety-nine percent of it was going to the dump.

"I only hope he really has moved on," Paul had told Betty, sitting in the basement flat that morning. "I'd love this to be a true clear-out, once and for all. I'd like to see him get into the swing of things and just get rid of much of it. I'm picturing a crocodile of people, passing junk along until it's thrown away."

"You think there really will be nothing worth saving?" Betty was making him tea and toast. He had refused her coffee, as usual, but accepted a cup of Earl Grey.

"Oh, I don't mean to be rude about Aunty's... about Doreen's things. But even those that did hold some value... they've disintegrated now, surely?" Paul said. She looked at him, and saw, as if for the first time, just how tired he was, following everything that had happened this year. This loyal young man. He worked hard, cared for his cousin, and carried the weight of it all on his shoulders.

"It will be lovely to have some time together, either way. Perhaps not so much while you are working, but it's been a while since we have had a barbecue and drinks. You know, I don't think April has ever been to one of our little socials, has she?"

"Oh no, she's only been here for the summer, and we've been a little lax this year. Last year we had several get-togethers, didn't we? Not so much this time. I guess... people haven't felt the urge," Paul said, absently. He was holding a piece of toast in his hand, cold and limp, now. He was looking away, drifting off into memories. Not all good, she supposed.

"Well then, we must make it a good one. For all of our sakes. I am thinking of sparkling wine and a few nice treats. And as for April – you know, I am very fond of that young lady. I want her to feel at home with us. Settled in. She's thoughtful and clever." She lowered her voice and leant forward towards him. "And you must have noticed, she's a pretty thing."

She saw his discomfort, which she took as a good sign. A shuffle of his feet; a slight blush. He looked to the toast and took an enthusiastic bite. Just as she had thought. There was something between them. Something that she hoped that the next night would solidify.

*

The last Friday of the month was the night when she spoke to Mark – as long as he wasn't out or busy. It had been two weeks since they had chatted last – two long weeks – and she was relieved when the phone rang at 7pm, as she knew it would be him. She was midway through pouring cake batter into tins at the time.

"Yay! I'm so glad you are in," he said as soon as she answered the phone.

"Where on Earth would I be, but here?" she laughed.

"Quite. Well. You took such a time to get to the phone, I was worried for a moment. It has been weeks since we talked. I thought it would be just my luck that you were out with some toyboy or something."

"No, he left an hour ago," she said.

160

He laughed down the phone – his deep, warm belly laugh that came so often and easily.

She looked over at the batter sitting in the cake tins and wondered whether to switch the oven off and accept that it would not be her best baking or to make him wait while she threw them in to cook.

"So, tell me – what's the news in Hummingbird House? How's the moody bugger on the top floor? And what's the new tenant like?"

She walked over to the oven and turned it off.

"Let me just get comfortable, and I shall tell you," she said.

Chapter Twenty-Nine
Betty (Then)

He walked across the room, and sat down opposite Sandra at the table, without saying a word. He dropped his bag to the floor, heavily, roughly loosened his tie, and then rubbed his face all over, with both hands. She noticed how his hair stood up in places, ruffled by the movement. She wanted to reach out to straighten it but stopped herself.

"It's only four-fifteen," Betty said, quietly.

William nodded, without looking at her. "Boss's birthday. There was a bit of a 'do'. I took the opportunity to sneak away."

"Right —"

"I knew you hadn't been *feeling well*, so I thought it would be a nice surprise." There was a tone to his voice that she didn't recognise. A sardonic, sharp one. His upper lip twisted as he spoke.

"Would you like me to leave?" Sandra asked, looking at Betty. She was frowning and shrunk down in her chair.

"Yes."

Sandra turned back towards him. "Actually, I was talking to Betty."

"Of course you were," he said. "You two are quite the pair these days, aren't you?"

"What on earth do you mean by that?" Sandra snapped.

"Stop," said Betty. "Stop now. We all need to start acting like grown-ups." She felt a tremor deep inside her as if her insides were cold. But she knew she had to find some strength to face this conversation.

"Sorry," Sandra said, reaching across to her. "I know."

"Let me go to get a drink and straighten my head a moment." William got up and walked to the kitchen in long strides. He shoved the doors behind him, and they swung back and forth, violently, settling into position, not quite shut.

"Stay with me," Betty said.

"Be strong," Sandra answered. "It'll be OK."

They could hear him, muttering to himself, though Betty couldn't decipher the words. Cupboard doors banged, and objects were set down hard, on the surface. Then silence, for a while, and she found herself holding her breath in anticipation of his return. But it was several minutes before he came back through. When he did, he seemed to have collected himself. He walked more slowly. His expression had softened.

"I... I apologise," he said, as he sat down again. He placed a mug on the table in front of him. It was one-third full of some sort of brown spirit. The sharp smell of alcohol cut through the air. "That was unnecessary and cruel. I don't know what came over me. Well, I do. A shock of sorts. Anyway, no excuses. Darling. Do you forgive me?" He turned to look at Betty for the first time.

"Of course I do." She looked back, relieved to see this change in him but desperate, yearning for more. He still had not touched her. He had not smiled. There was a pinch between his brows.

He had not said he was pleased.

"Tell me everything," he said. "I heard the main news, but only the headline, as it were. How long have you known? Are you well?"

"Only nausea. The doctor says I'm well."

"The doctor?"

"I saw a doctor today. It was only today that I found out. I haven't been keeping a big secret from you, I promise. Only that I was late. I didn't even suspect anything until a few days ago. Even then…" She trailed off.

"What did the doctor say?" He took a large gulp of his drink.

"She said —"

"She?" He raised an eyebrow.

"Yes. My usual doctor is on holiday, so I saw someone else. She examined me and asked some questions. I have all the symptoms. She's made a referral for maternity checks."

"What symptoms?" he asked, quickly. He took another gulp.

"The usual… darling, do you really want to know all the details?" She wriggled in the chair.

"Yes, tell me. Nothing can shock me further today."

She took a breath. "I am late by nine or ten days, which is a lot. We had… I've been nauseated without reason. I have, well, I'm tender. I've been feeling the heat a lot, tired. And we did have… relations at the time of the month when you are most likely to conceive."

She looked to Sandra for reassurance, as this comment had originally come from her, but then realised how inappropriate she was. Lord knows what William would think of them discussing what went on in the bedroom, together. She glanced away.

He said nothing so they sat in silence for a moment while he sipped from his mug. He was still and calm now, ostensibly, but who knew what he was holding under the surface; what his thoughts were? Betty wanted to say more – something that might reassure him – but was at a loss.

"Tea?" Sandra asked.

"OK," Betty answered. William didn't respond. He continued to stare down into his mug and take regular sips.

For three or four minutes they sat at the table close to each other, but not touching, as the sounds of Sandra lighting the stove and boiling the kettle, then making a pot of tea, could be heard in the background.

When Sandra returned, the noise of her chair as she pulled it from the table seemed to snap him out of his thoughts.

"It's silly really, but I somehow never thought this would happen. I don't know what I expected. But I didn't think we'd be here, having this conversation. At least, not so soon into the marriage." He spoke softly, as if to himself.

"But why?" she asked, turning to him. "I thought the opposite. That it would be quick, planned, and loved. I'm twenty-eight." Betty said. She didn't know what to say to comfort or persuade him, because she had no understanding of what could be going on in his head. But she genuinely wanted to know.

"Yes, but perhaps that's part of it."

"What do you mean?" she asked.

"You're twenty-eight. I thought… you're older. You've never particularly shown an interest in… this. And I thought maybe it wouldn't happen anyway. Because of our ages."

"Are you…" Betty felt tears begin to prick again. Not now. Not now. She needed to remain collected. "Are you saying you married me because I am *old*?"

"God, no, darling." He looked at her, mortified. It was the first time he had truly looked into her eyes. "Of course not. I love you. I love you for who you are."

"But it's part of the appeal though, is it? Or at least, you thought I didn't want children, seeing as I had lasted this long without them. Like some sort of *old maid*?"

"I hate that expression," Sandra muttered, bitterly.

"No, of course not. Not exactly. I just thought it was something else we had in common. That we are of a similar mindset, a similar age, so we were past that sort of thing."

"Past it?"

"Yes. I have my career. You're doing up the house. We have a lovely home. Tenants, too." He glanced at Sandra. "We might even make something of that. There's always the top floor. Anyway, I thought we were settled down and looking forward to a comfortable middle age."

"Ha!" Sandra spat. "Sorry, I know this is really between you two, but I just can't stand it. You're

166

talking like… She's twenty-eight, not eighty-two. She has years to come, yet."

Chapter Thirty
Betty (Now)

Betty dressed upon waking – before she had even had breakfast. No dawdling. She would shower later. Today she wanted to be alert and active. Productive. It was the day of the barbecue. This was energising, really. She did like to entertain; vowed to do it more often. Perhaps she should put the dates in the calendar now – not to let things slide for so long next time.

She had food to prep, wine to buy, cakes to ice, and relationships to encourage.

She decided to have a glass of orange juice and go straight to the shop. She made herself a list and then put on her red court shoes, grabbed her hessian bag and climbed the stairs to exit via the front door.

On the landing she paused, wondering if it was too early to knock on Jonty and Ben's door to see if they had any last-minute groceries they needed for later. It was only 8:30 am, and she knew they sometimes stayed in bed late on the weekend. She had thought better of knocking on their door when she heard a snippet of music, so she risked it. Besides, she had already seen Oxo, which implied somebody was awake, at least.

Ben answered. "Betty, what can I do for you on this beautiful morning?"

"Is it? I haven't even looked out the window yet," Betty said.

"It is indeed. I've just been out for a quick run. Well, jog might be a more accurate way of putting it. It's going to be a lovely day."

Betty smiled. She had never known Ben to jog but thought it unbecoming to comment on it. "I am off to the shop and wondered if you might need anything for tonight."

"No, I should say not. He cleared the shelves in the supermarket yesterday." Ben gestured into the depths of the flat with one thumb. "We have a kitchen full of bread rolls and burgers."

"That's what I like to hear. I'll just get some nibbles and strawberries. And wine, I suppose."

"Oh, hang on. There is something, actually. His mother is down tomorrow – did you know? We've finally managed to drag her away from her role as the local village troublemaker for a week or so. She only relented a couple of days ago. Anyway, she comes tomorrow – strike while the iron is hot. She only drinks Peppermint Tea. It's the one bloody thing we forgot, of course. Could you pick some up? Only if you remember."

"I didn't know. Well, how lovely."

"One way of putting it!" He rolled his eyes to the heavens, melodramatically. "Him indoors is catching up on his sleep before she gets here. There'll be no rest for the wicked, once she does."

"This is turning out to be rather an action-packed weekend, isn't it?" she said.

"Fingers crossed nothing *too* action-packed. No fainting or fires. I'm hoping for a bit of quiet life for a while. I've had enough drama for one summer."

169

"You may just have to wait one more week, in that case," Betty answered, with a smile.

Chapter Thirty-One
Betty (Then)

It was six-thirty. They had been sitting at the table for over two hours. Betty had drunk a gallon of tea, and eaten a piece of toast, unenthusiastically, at Sandra's insistence. William had asked her repeatedly about the doctor's appointment, and about what would happen next. Betty wasn't entirely sure but tried to respond with confidence, not wanting to create room for angst. He asked about risks for older mothers; when the baby would be due; how old Dorothy had been when she had her brother. At one stage, he seemed to be suggesting they should get a second opinion.

"Because she saw a female doctor, I suppose?" Sandra asked, chin out. He didn't push it any further.

And there were long lapses where they said nothing at all. Sometimes Betty would cry, and Sandra would comfort her, but William did not. He seemed unaware. Absorbed. He continued to stare at the table, or his mug. Occasionally, he topped it up.

"I feel as if we are dancing around this, and it doesn't sit well with me. Can we be very clear then, and place all our cards on the table?" Sandra asked.

"What do you mean?" Betty responded, through a sniff.

Sandra rapped the table in front of William. "You never wanted children and you still don't. And you told yourself that Betty didn't either. And you're both bloody old and knackered, so it would never happen anyway. Right?"

William winced and kept his eyes closed. He had crossed one leg over another and was bent forward, rocking gently.

"Right?" she asked again, with more force.

"Yes," he said. "I have never wanted children. And I'm a fool for not telling you before, I know that." He turned to face her, his eyes still closed, face reddened, in some monstrous representation of her husband, her darling William, the man she loved.

"But you do, Betty. You do want children. And if it wasn't for…" She paused, sneering in his direction. "*Him*, you'd be happy about this. Is that correct?"

"Yes," she said, after a beat.

"Then I think you'd best decide what you're going to do next."

William opened his eyes – then fluttered them in a series of sharp blinks as if waking or wading through smoke.

"Yes, but what can we do? It's happened now. It's a bit late to be talking about plans, or contraceptives."

"On the contrary," Sandra said, holding up one hand. "I think you have several options. One, you can hang on and do nothing." She tapped her index finger. "Lots of pregnancies end in miscarriage, you know. It happened to a good friend of mine. You are in the early stages. It could happen to you. I

172

don't mean to sound heartless, but perhaps we are all feeling angst over nothing."

Betty noticed William nodding fiercely, and humming 'Mmm' as if this was very sage advice – happy in the knowledge that this pregnancy might end in loss. Who was this man? She found herself gripping the edge of the table with both hands.

"Two, William makes a concerted effort to step up to this situation." Sandra leant forward slightly, pushing her middle finger down, backwards, so far in his direction that it was bent over on itself. "After all, it takes two to tango." This time it was Betty who was nodding. "Three, one of you moves out. Or four —"

"Wait a minute! What do you mean by that? You want us to get divorced?" Betty asked, aghast. This had never occurred to her.

"We will not!" William said. "Never in a million years."

"It's good to see a strong reaction from you for once, William. At least we now know you want your marriage to work. But no, I didn't say divorce, did I? It doesn't have to be permanent or legal. I was suggesting that you both might be better living apart if you have conflicting opinions on raising a child."

William pushed himself away from the table, as if to distance himself from her – to create a space between himself and the idea, perhaps. "Don't be ridiculous."

"Me?" Sandra asked, tilting her head, and staring at him with raised brows.

"What was four?" Betty asked.

Sandra held up her hand again, with four fingers up. She pinched her little finger tightly and wiggled it back and forth. "Four, you have an abortion."

"What?" Betty stood up quickly and her chair toppled over behind her. She ignored it. "I can't believe you would even suggest that."

Sandra stood too, and picked up Betty's chair, gently pushing Betty by the shoulder to resume her seat, shushing and stroking her. "Sorry, Betty, sorry. I… I am never tactful, you know me. Perhaps that could have been done with a bit of verbal cushioning. I am saying it because it's an option. Only one option. And you need to consider everything. I didn't mean to… Come on. Sit down."

"It's still illegal, isn't it?" William said. "I know Steel has proposed it but it's not in law yet. I'm right, aren't I? So, this really isn't an option at all. I'm not sure why you feel the need to bring it up."

Betty could feel her thoughts collapsing, one on top of the other, like a stack of cards. They were tumbling and she could not catch them. Everything was descending into chaos in her mind. Around her. She couldn't think properly. She couldn't speak.

"It'll be through soon enough," Sandra said, directly.

"Soon enough… soon enough for…" William looked at Betty.

"Well, no, perhaps not. I just meant it's barely illegal. It's almost passed."

"Either something is legal or it's not," William said.

"I know. Look, I didn't mean to upset you both. I'm honestly trying to help. But if you did want to think about it… if you do consider it to be one of your options, then I may be able to assist."

"You?" he asked.

"I know someone," was all she said in reply.

*

Betty lay in the bath. She hadn't really known what else to do. She wanted to clean away the conversation they had had, and she needed an excuse to be alone, away from William. He had run the bath for her, adding bath salts and placing a clean towel on the hook on the back of the door. But he had done it silently, automatically. He still had not touched her. Not once.

Shortly after she had relayed her list of options to them, Sandra had gone downstairs. By then it was early evening, and Robert would have been wondering where she was, she said. Besides, they were all exhausted. Fraught. Betty's eyes felt swollen and tender. William had drunk several mugs of whatever brown liquid he had periodically replenished.

It still felt unreal. Lying in the bath, she glanced down at her tummy beneath the milky water. It looked the same as always. Slim, but not what you would call thin. She had a small pouch of a tummy below her belly button. It was hard to process that there was a baby – an embryo – growing within.

And that William did not want it.

There was a knock on the bathroom door. She jumped slightly and sat up. For a moment, she considered covering her body with her hands, or a towel, even though it could only be William.

"I'm going for a walk," he said through the door. His voice was flat.

It was eight o'clock at night, though the summer nights were still long. It was not yet dusk.

"OK," she said.

Silence. She was unsure if he was still there and thought perhaps he had gone without saying another word. "Do you need anything?" he asked, after a while.

"No, thank you," she replied, wincing at the awkwardness – the formality with which they spoke.

"See you in about an hour, I suppose," he said. And then she heard his footsteps as he walked away.

She stayed in the bath long after the water had started to cool. She allowed herself to daydream; to picture a number of possible outcomes. William happy, playing with a toddler, perhaps even having a second baby on the way. It was possible. He might come around. Or William as he had just been; formal, tight, withdrawn, as she tended to the baby and he sat in his chair, drinking whisky from a mug. William angry: shouting at her and the child. Smashing plates in the kitchen. Never forgiving her for what she had brought into his life.

What was to be?

She realised the skin on her upper chest was prickled with goosebumps, so cold was the water. Now was the time to get out before she made herself ill. She pulled the plug out and stood, cautiously, taking the towel he had left her and drying herself roughly before she made her way into their bedroom where she pulled out the same comfortable nightgown she had worn on the day she had discussed the pregnancy with Sandra.

176

She lay down on the bed – on top of the covers – and within fifteen minutes, she was asleep.

*

She felt something draped across her. Confused, she opened her eyes. Unsure where she was at first, and what had happened, she slowly realised she was still in her bedroom but that it was dark, late, and someone else was there. William. He was sitting on the edge of the bed, staring at her.

She propped herself up with one arm and tried to focus. "What is it?" she asked. "I mean – what time is it?"

"Late," he said. "You should go back to sleep." He spoke in a half-whisper. "Sorry if I woke you. I didn't want you to be cold."

She looked down and realised he had placed a blanket on her. It was old, pink, and a little dusty. She wondered where he had found it. She didn't even recognise it.

"Thanks," she said, still propped up. "How are you?" It was a futile question, she knew. There was no way he had changed all of his feelings in the space of a couple of hours, but she could not help but hope. Besides, she cared about him. She didn't want to see him in pain.

"I'm OK. Over the initial shock, I think."

She nodded. "I'm sorry you found out that way. You know that was never my intention."

"Of course," he said. He slipped off his shoes. Her eyes were starting to adjust to the light, and she could see him now. See how tired he looked. How strained.

"Have you… have you had any more thoughts?" he said. "About the future. About how you feel about it all?"

"Only in relation to you. Everything hinges on you, and your feelings, doesn't it? You're the one in control."

He chuckled. "In control. Am I?" He shook his head.

"We'll talk about it tomorrow. Or maybe… maybe in a couple of days? Let it sink in a bit further." She reached over as if to stroke his arm but stopped herself. She wasn't sure how he would respond.

"I think we should consider option four," he stated.

For a moment she was confused, unable to recall what numbers correlated with each suggestion. Four.

"Four?"

"I think we should talk to someone about having an abortion."

Chapter Thirty-Two
Betty (Now)

Jonty and Ben arrived first, arms laden with food and a bag of charcoal briquettes. Pleased to see that Betty had made a Strawberry Shortcake, Jonty went to pull his car around to the rear of the house while Ben helped Betty in the kitchen. Jonty had lined the boot with tarpaulin and an old sheet which he then left open, ready to receive any and all of the waste they'd be dumping from the remnants of the shed. The two men went straight to work, clearing the garden.

April and David arrived after a while. Betty was delighted to see them sporting new haircuts. David was even clean-shaven. His hair was tightly cropped at the back and sides in the way that many young men had it these days – not to her taste, but it did make him appear fresher and younger. His beaming smile told her that her instinct had been right – it had done David the world of good to be groomed and spend a day out with April. The pair of them bowed to the rapturous applause they were met with.

April's hair was sleek and shiny, much shorter than it had been, and poker-straight. Betty watched as she repeatedly flicked her hair, ostensibly as a joke, though she seemed secretly pleased with the outcome of this trip to the stylist.

Then it was Paul's turn to arrive and the whole of Hummingbird House was together, for once. She watched as his eyes searched for April, immediately, and the grin that appeared on his face at the sight of her. Paul had invited along one of the young women from the neighbourhood – Rosie – the one with the fruit and vegetable box. They were on nodding terms only, so it was rather lovely to have her there, as it meant Betty would finally get to know her, though she had not brought along the young woman she lived with. Plus, she was secretly relieved as having a relative stranger among them made it even less likely that David would cause any sort of scene.

The crew worked diligently, sifting through mud, damp wood, and ash, to unearth a handful of precious items to keep. A photograph. Some dumbbells. A necklace. But, just as Paul had predicted, much of the contents of the shed had been utterly destroyed and were placed in the boot of the car for the dump.

The car dipped under the weight of the debris. The things at the back of the shed had not all been burnt in their entirety, but they were sodden as they had been doused by the Fire Brigade. The items at the front had been ablaze and they were hard-pressed to even identify what they had once been. Betty watched as Doreen's things fell apart upon lifting, turning to mulch in their hands. David appeared to be handling it remarkably well – his army of loyal supporters beside him. Periodically, Paul would crack a joke, or Jonty would slap him affectionately across the shoulders.

As time went on, Betty called Ben away to help

set start the barbecue coals. She noticed that the car was full, now, and the tenants were piling bin bags against the wall for a second trip. What would she do without these wholesome, helpful young people?

"That's enough," she called to them, doing her best to sound assertive. "Please. Leave it be. You really have done the lion's share. There'll be nothing left for the landscaper to do, at this rate. And he charges a fortune."

"Landscaper?" April asked her, confused.

"Yes, I have some fancy garden designer coming this week to talk to me about a new patio and shed. And a few other bits and pieces. I've never used anyone like that in my life, but I thought I'd use this as an excuse to tidy everything up."

"Will the insurance pay out, Betty? Would you like me to chase them up for you?" It was David, a pinch of worry and guilt on his face again.

"Please, no more work and no more money talk. Time to rehydrate you. And I have just the thing," she said, turning on her heel to collect wine glasses from the kitchen.

"Did someone say drink?" Jonty called over.

"Yes, just the kind you like. I gather it's the only way I can be certain that you workers will stop," she said. "But I want to see you wash up, first."

She watched them dutifully do as instructed, no doubt relieved to have an excuse to break. She placed the glasses on the garden table and collected the bottle of sparkling wine that she had bought for the occasion. She hoped that the hard labour and the forthcoming good food would set a comfortable tone for the rest of the evening. Things were working out nicely.

"Would you open this for me, Paul?" she said. "I can always rely on you."

Chapter Thirty-Three
Betty (Then)

William had wasted no time. The next morning, he brought up the subject again, over breakfast. And then once more, at dinner. She placed a plate before him, and the moment she sat he looked at her, unblinking, and asked what her thoughts were. She knew it was coming, yet still could find no words. He was calm, and logical, and promised that this was an exploration of the idea, nothing more. One possible solution.

Abortion.

Betty had never thought that her pregnancy would be a problem that needed resolving.

It wasn't that she disagreed with it, per se. It seemed frightening. And somehow brutal. Though it was more that she had not imagined it was something that would ever feature in her own life. She wasn't completely naïve – she didn't know anyone who had completed an abortion but she was fully aware that they happened. And she had heard stories, second-hand. A girl from school, in the year above. A friend of a friend at work. But these were other people's relatives and friends. Other people's lives. Not a married twenty-eight-year-old with a wished-for baby.

Did these things happen to people like her? Extraordinarily, painfully, it seemed perhaps they did.

Eventually, by Wednesday morning when he had returned to the topic again, and again, she had started to feel foolish. Stubborn, perhaps, that she would not countenance a discussion. She was tired and scared of what would happen if she continued to say no. She was scared of what would happen to her marriage.

As soon as Betty had agreed to discuss the abortion – no promises – he had been downstairs to ask Sandra for her help.

Sandra didn't know a doctor, per se, but she knew someone who did. A friend of hers from art college, Rahmi. She had an abortion about six months ago and Sandra was certain she'd be happy to talk about what it entailed or to pass on the doctor's contact details, as she had no regrets. They had settled on a visit from Rahmi the coming Friday if she could make it. Talking to a doctor was a step too far. This, she could cope with – just. Betty asked Sandra if she would stay with them when they met. She didn't ask William and he did not offer.

In the time leading up to her visit, Betty was plagued with irrational fears that this would lead to a police raid or her arrest. She fretted that Rahmi would be bugged, or followed, and the whole thing would be some form of a malicious sting operation. She knew it was ludicrous, but at the same time, it was odd to think they were wilfully exploring something illegal. Something taboo. She slept poorly and although she no longer felt sick on and off, she felt exhausted and uncomfortable,

184

sometimes accompanied by fleeting stabbing pains in her abdomen, which she was sure came from stress.

*

On Thursday evening, the day before Rahmi's visit, there was a knock on the sitting room door. William was already home and was sitting in his chair, dozing slightly. Betty was in the kitchen, preparing chops and potatoes for dinner, listening to her transistor, with the volume on low. She rushed to the door, assuming it was Sandra, and concerned she might come in and awaken him.

It was Nigel. "Little sis!" he cried when she opened the door. She launched herself at him and enveloped him in a hug. He reciprocated. She had surprised herself and felt a touch ridiculous but he didn't seem at all fazed.

"You are so quiet up here, that Sandy said she thought you'd gone out but I wanted to check for myself. And here you are!"

She pulled him in by his coat sleeve and placed a finger on her lips, gesturing to William with the other hand. He closed the door behind him.

"Now I see why," he whispered.

Continuing to hang onto his sleeve, she walked him through the room to the kitchen, where she closed the doors behind them.

"Poor old man," he said, smiling. "You've been working him too hard."

"It's been a tough week," she said. He nodded, and she wondered if Sandra had told him anything. She hoped not.

"Let me finish dinner but I want to hear your news. Tell me something to take my mind off the horrid time we've been having."

"Make me a cup of tea, and I shall oblige," he said.

*

Half an hour later, Nigel was mid-way through a ridiculous story about a former colleague who thought his name was Neville for several years, and all the confusion this entailed, when William opened the door. For a moment she was concerned, worried he would be upset that they had woken him, but he grinned at the sight of Nigel, and for the first time since Monday, he came over and kissed her on the cheek.

"I thought it was you," William said, leaning forward to shake his hand. "Sorry not to have given you a more rapturous welcome."

"Oh, I am the one who has been imposing. Anyway, I must get downstairs to Sandy. She was making me a curry, apparently."

"Curry! Can't say that I have tried it, myself."

"I have had one or two. A friend from work is from Bangladesh and his brother has a restaurant. I am apprehensive about a home-cooked version from Sandy but I'll try anything once." He winked at William, who simply laughed in response.

"Right, you two lovebirds, we must get a date in the calendar to catch up. Perhaps we could even venture out, sometime. My treat."

"I shall hold you to that," William replied, leaning forward to take a piece of raw carrot from the saucepan.

"Oh! We can go for a curry. That's settled, then."

*

Whether from the nap, the visitor, or the forthcoming meeting with Rahmi, William was more relaxed and chirpy than he had been all week. He complimented her dinner and ate ravenously. He asked her how she was feeling. He told her about work and a possible new project he was to be involved in; it might even lead to a promotion.

Betty ate little again but this time more from anxiety than nausea. She was relieved to see the change in him. She offered him her plate, which he took readily after he had cleared his own. She sat, quietly, and listened to him talk, passing him condiments and filling his glass wordlessly. Things almost seemed normal once more, so she was scared to move too quickly, say too much, or trigger something to rock the boat.

When he had finished his second helping, she reached over to take the plate away and he grabbed her wrist, unexpectedly. She looked down at his delicate, long fingers encircling her arm.

"Darling, you do know I love you, don't you?"

She could not meet his eyes. "Of course," she said.

"It's not to do with how I feel about you. And I know I'm a fool, and I should have shared this with you. I know I haven't been open with you. And I can't even explain why it's such an issue for me. But it is. I'm sorry, but it is. I have caused you pain. And I hate that. Hate that." His voice cracked at this.

She leant back in her chair again and he released his grip on her. "Is there anything else, William?" She regretted it as soon as she said it.

"What do you mean?" He seemed genuinely confused.

"Nothing. Sorry. I don't know why I said that." She made to move away again.

"No – stop. Tell me what you meant?" His voice was more assertive, this time.

She paused, then answered. "Anything else you haven't told me."

"I — no. Honestly. Why do you ask?"

Betty hesitated, unsure how to continue. She wasn't even sure what it was he could be hiding. But she felt there was something. There had to be something. She found herself picking at the skin on her thumb again, curling her arms in a bundle before her, almost hugging herself. She wanted to feel pressure, and touch on her skin. She wanted to feel loved.

"The time we made love, that was the day we went to dinner downstairs. And then… and then the next time we had Sunday lunch with them," she gestured downwards, "I got the impression that you were keen to… to…"

"But what do you mean? Why is that an issue? I don't even remember."

"Just now, again. When Nigel has been here. It's rather perked you up. I wondered if you…"

"If I what?" he asked. "Just say it, darling."

"If you fancied them," she said, feeling foolish at her own words.

188

William laughed, apparently taken aback. "Fancied them? Fancied who, exactly? Our tenants? *Nigel?*"

"Maybe."

His laughter dissipated. He stared at the table for a beat. "Nigel wasn't at the meal on that night, remember? You're reading things into it that simply aren't there. It was you I wanted."

"Do you, though? Do you really? Because it seems to me that you're very good at cuddles and pecks on the cheek but rather less fond of anything remotely sexual."

She looked up at him and saw his face – wounded, aghast. He reeled back at her words, harsh and flat as they were. She hadn't planned to say them. Hadn't even truly known her own thoughts until she did.

They sat in silence for a moment and then she picked up the plates. This time he did not stop her. She poured herself a glass of water in the kitchen, stalling, avoiding a return to the room. She didn't want to face the fallout from what she had said.

When she did, he was sitting in exactly the same place, still, even his hands remained flat on the table as they had been. She sat opposite him again. She needed to be brave.

"It's funny," he said, suddenly. "I thought the same of you."

"I… That I fancied Nigel?"

"Sandra. That you were attracted to her."

"What?" Betty felt her thoughts, both speeding up and slowing concurrently. Cogs and wheels and trains of thought that she could not catch. She had never thought about women in that way. Or that

189

other women did. Did they? Yes, they must. Some of them. "I don't believe it. Whatever gave you that idea?"

"Oh, you know. Just the blushing whenever she is around. The adulation. The nerves. I've never seen you so concerned about your appearance." He shrugged.

He was right. She did do all those things. She did act that way. She considered: perhaps it was understandable that this may cross his mind. If she could think this of him and expect an honest response, then why shouldn't he think the same?

She took three deep breaths to collect herself.

No, she wasn't attracted to her – infatuated, perhaps, at the start, but not in a sexual way. She knew how she felt about William – how she felt her body tense, her heart flutter like a caged bird when he touched her. It was not the same. She felt nervous, and panicked even, around her at the beginning, but the thought of love, or romance, or sex – that just didn't fit neatly with the way that she felt towards her.

"OK. I can see that. I can see why you would say it. I think it was a sort of schoolgirl crush. I didn't want her but I wanted to be her. It's passed, now. Gosh, I am pathetic, really."

"You don't spend enough time with other people," he said. "You've not seen any of your old friends for months. It's not good for one to be cloistered away."

This was true, she realised. She had seen no one. Not her old friends from school; not her ex-colleagues; not even her brother. Her mother, a few times, and Sandra. That was all. It was not intentional but there was no denying it.

"You're right. But you haven't answered me, William. Please. Is there something else? Are you attracted to someone else? Or – I don't know – is there something you're not telling me? Something that's happened in the past or…"

He didn't answer and gave a brief shake of his head. She was unconvinced and forced herself to persist; she had come this far. It would be easiest to leave this conversation now, raw and embarrassing as it had already been, but she knew they would never talk of it again if they did.

The bottom of her back was complaining about how long she had been sitting on the hard chair. Her stomach flipped. But she needed to ignore it and push through.

"When we were first together," she continued. "I thought we were so close that we had a unique connection. It was nothing I'd ever felt or imagined. As if I could tell what you thought and felt and I didn't even need to say. Absolute pure trust. Absolute unity. And then we married, and after a little while, I realised that there must be something there. Something I hadn't spotted. And now I'm sure that there is a feeling you have, or a doubt, or a secret, and I have no idea what it is, or how to make you share it with me. But I wish you would. I only wish you would."

"But there is no secret. Nothing has happened. And there is no feeling I can put into words."

"Try."

"OK," he said. "OK, I will." He looked up at her, and she could see a new nervousness in him,

191

and anxiety that was rarely there. "I think… the reason it happened that night was that I love you, and I could see how happy you were, and I wanted to keep you happy and to share that happiness and it just sort of took me over. And I do think you are beautiful. And I do love you."

"But what?" she asked. "What is the catch?"

"But I just don't often feel that way. At all. About anyone."

"I don't understand," she said.

"That makes two of us," he said. "I don't really know how else to explain it but I have been aware of it… for years, I suppose. Since school. I don't often have that urge, and it is impossible to force, or fake. When I look at you, I see the beauty and the person that you are. And I want to touch you, to hold you, to keep you close. But I don't think it's the same as what… as what other men – no, maybe just other people, feel. It doesn't seem that way. Unless everyone else is faking things, too."

"I — right. OK," she said, tentatively. She wasn't sure how to proceed, or what this meant. But she was glad that he was talking to her, at least.

"I know it is a cliché to say that 'it's not you', but it really isn't, as for me it is not anyone. I don't really fancy anyone. No one at all. Not in the way it seems that other chaps do. But in my own way, I…"

She looked at him, the pleading in his eyes. The nervousness, no, the fear on his face. He looked wretched, twisted. Ashamed. But he loved her. He did love her.

"I guess it's what you would call a low libido?" He whispered the words into his own shoulder, as

192

he curled forward and buried his face in his right arm.

"OK," she said, again. There were no good words with which to respond to this. Or none that she knew.

"I had imagined I would stay alone, to be honest. I didn't think I would marry. You are the closest I have come to it – to that *normal* romantic feeling, as I imagine it to be, at least. And sometimes I thought that if I ignored my issues, they would slowly fall away, and it would all turn into what everyone else has. Sort of evolving over time. And other times I thought if I ignored them, eventually you would, too. And this would be our normal. That you would accept it."

They both sat for a beat in the silence. She could feel the blood in her ears; feel a tingling across her face. Then she spoke.

"Stop. You don't have to worry. I understand, I think. Or I will try to." She wanted to. She wanted him more than anything else, so she would have to make this work.

"And I definitely don't fancy bloody *Nigel*." He pulled a face in an attempt to make her laugh. She smiled at him.

"Let me make you some tea," he said. "You hardly ate anything. You can't survive on carrots alone."

"OK," she said. "I do feel a bit odd. Tea sounds good. Let's go over to the sitting room."

He kissed the top of her head as he went past her, to the kitchen.

She stood, and found herself light-headed, so gripped the back of the chair briefly. The nausea was back. She steadied herself, breathing slowly, trying to slow her racing heart. She glanced down. And there, on the white plastic seat, was a speck of crimson blood.

Chapter Thirty-Four
Betty (Now)

She collected empty plates and serviettes as unobtrusively as possible, weaving between her guests and carefully treading the path to the kitchen, back and forth. The path had always been uneven and rustic, but the footfall and recent incident made it frankly hazardous in places, now. She was glad to have made the decision to hire someone to work on it. Besides, she needed something easy to maintain. She placed more wine in front of Jonty. He smiled up at her.

Rosie was talking – she was a bold young woman, captivating to listen to, though Betty winced at her candour with her audience, some of whom she hardly knew. Whether this was the result of the wine or her personality, it was hard to tell.

Rosie sat in a chair, knees bent, bare feet up on the cushion. She talked about her marriage – long over, although she could not have been much more than thirty. She had been wed to an older man, straight from university, after they had quickly and powerfully fallen in love. But they had not been able to have a child – and the journey they had been on together had resulted in them walking down two different paths. She talked about medication, sickness, scans, arguments, hope, and loss.

For a moment, Betty felt a pang. She didn't often

think back on those days. On her own lost baby. The fierce, hot pressure it had placed her and William under. She had hardly spoken of it with anyone, even at the time. She was almost jealous of the ease with which this Rosie relayed her events and the fact that Betty could not bring herself to do the same. But at the same time, she also felt there was something special in keeping it to herself. A reverence. Anyway, it was too late, now. It was all too late.

The table was clear and Betty loitered nearby, briefly. She wondered if she could slip away yet. But there was no chance of that as once spotted, there was a tussle of sorts as each of the young people offered her a seat, insisting she took it. She declined Paul's offer, worried that if he remained standing, this might encourage him to leave early, which would never do. Though when April stood, she accepted, gladly watching as she took herself over and perched on the arm of the bench, next to Paul, leaning back against him.

Encouraged by her proximity, Betty noticed how he touched her arm and her back, periodically, gently, as if marvelling at her. In awe. Then eventually April slid down next to him on the seat, squeezing into the tiny space beside him, so that they were tight, warm, and cosy together. Just as she had hoped.

Chapter Thirty-Five
Betty (Then)

By eight o'clock she had started to bleed more heavily. William tried to reassure her, though the irony of him comforting her when she knew how he felt about the pregnancy was not lost on either of them.

Betty waited for him to suggest a trip to the hospital but he did not. She wondered if it was foolish to consider it. What would most people do? She had no idea. She didn't ask; thought he would know, for some reason. This was William. He always knew what to say or do.

"It's been a very big week for you," William said, as he squatted down beside her where she lay on the sofa. He had opened all the doors and windows at her request. "It's hardly surprising you don't feel wonderful."

"But blood, William. I am bleeding. When has blood ever been a good sign?" she asked, desperate for an answer.

He kissed her forehead. "Shall we get you upstairs? Perhaps a night of sleep will help."

"Sleep?" How could she sleep? Her mind was a pinball machine, her lower back cramping intensely, on and off.

"Bed would be more comfortable, I think. I could get you something. Aspirin? Brandy? What would help?"

"Do you think… maybe the doctor?" She moved to sit up and he lowered one hand down to her to help her to stand.

"I'm not sure what they can do in these circumstances. I suspect bed rest is the treatment."

They started to walk together towards the sitting room door, she leant against him, glad to feel his hard muscles against her, for once. The warmth of him. They had not been close to one another for days.

"Will you stay with me for a while?" she asked.

"Of course," he said, smiling down at her. "And if you still feel unwell in the morning, we will go to the surgery first thing. Does that sound like a plan?"

*

"I want to see Doctor Janus," Betty said. It was a different receptionist, this time. She looked up at her and frowned.

Betty had been queuing at the glass doors of the reception for several minutes already and badly needed to sit. Friday morning was clearly a busy time at the surgery. William was parking the car.

"Doctor Janus doesn't have any free appointments today. You can get one for next week… Tuesday?" The woman was flicking ahead in the appointment book, pen in hand, ready to book her in.

"No, this is… I need to see her today. I need to see her soon."

"If it's urgent, I do have some space with another doctor. I can give you Doctor —"

"No. Janus. Doctor Janus. I want to see Doctor Janus." She leant against the glass.

"Doctor Janus doesn't have any spare appointments." The receptionist closed the book, firmly and looked at her. She was visibly irritated.

"But I need —"

"What's going on, here?" It was William, by her side. He held her by the elbow.

"She says there are no appointments." She felt her eyes brimming with tears but she didn't care.

"Come here," William said. He folded his arms around her. She was unsure what was happening, where they were going, as they crab-walked together, awkwardly. He took her into the waiting room.

He helped her to sit. "Wait here," he said. "Let me sort it out."

She nodded and watched him leave her there. It was only after she saw him disappear through the doorway that she realised that the room was full: an elderly couple sat together; a mother with three children; a man in a pin-striped suit. They were all silent. Staring, as she sat in the middle of them.

*

Somehow, William had convinced the receptionist to allow Betty to be on standby for cancellations or no-shows. She wondered how it was that this option suddenly became available when it had not been given to her, but in the end, was simply grateful to know she would be seen.

She only had to wait twenty minutes. Doctor Janus appeared in the doorway and called her name, and, when she saw her, slumped as she was against William, she came across the room to fetch her. William helped her to stand and checked she was fine to walk with the doctor, then sat back down.

"Wouldn't you like to come in, too, Mr Williams?" Doctor Janus said. It didn't sound truly as if this were a question. As if she expected him to relent, and follow them in.

William shrugged this off. "No, thank you. I am confident she's in capable hands."

She didn't answer but looked at him for a beat longer before turning away again and walking with Betty to her room.

*

She was in the hospital for three nights. It was a 'spontaneous abortion' they said.

The amount of blood she had lost – and continued to lose – meant they said it was safest to admit her.

Doctor Janus thought she had already lost the baby by the time she saw her; the amount of blood she was still shedding suggested there was nothing anyone could do. It was more common than she thought, apparently. One in four pregnancies or perhaps higher. Betty thought of all the women she knew, finding herself mentally counting them up in her head and wondering which of them had experienced this. None of them had said.

The hospital stay was a precaution. Routinely, it would be two nights, they explained – but that would involve a Sunday discharge that the doctors weren't keen on. William was instructed to leave her there and collect her on Monday morning.

Betty wanted to understand. Why did she need to be here rather than at home, in her own bed? If there was nothing they could do, why couldn't she go home? It was possible to develop an infection or to lose more blood, she was told. Or occasionally, women would have an 'incomplete abortion', leading to a haemorrhage. So she needed to be careful. Betty was thankful to have seen Doctor Janus who explained it all to her, in her calm but matter-of-fact tones, as once she was in the hospital she was hardly spoken to at all.

She was given an enema and a bath on arrival, then placed on bed rest for the first twenty-four hours. Ironically, the nurses then opening the curtains at half past six each morning, religiously, when she could easily have remained asleep. She would lie still, sheets tucked up to her chin, staring at the high, greying ceiling and listening to the clack of shoes on the vinyl floor. The nurses were brusque, starched, and matter-of-fact. There was no time for chatter. She stayed in silence except for meal times, when they tried to feed her red meat and cabbage and chastised her when she didn't finish.

The entire process made her feel like a naughty girl.

She couldn't wait to go home. She counted the hours that she sat up in bed, alone save for the odd conversation with other women. The atmosphere was bleak. The walls white. The floor was old and discoloured. When she did leave, finally, her legs wobbled beneath her and her clothes felt stiff and heavy.

William was there, having taken a day off work. He joked with the nurses and the elderly man who swept the floor. He carried her bag as they walked together, slowly, back to the car – past the nursery full of new-born babes who could be seen through the glass: a wriggling wall of limbs dressed in pink, blue, yellow and white woollen hats, with doting fathers staring at them in awe.

*

Betty took herself to bed. She didn't know what else to do. She told William she had cramps, though it wasn't true, and that the hospital had ordered her to rest in peace and quiet for a couple of weeks. She saw the look on his face as she said so. It was relief.

For the first twenty-four hours, she stayed in silence, alone. William slept elsewhere – the sofa, she assumed. He brought her tea and toast for breakfast, lunch and dinner, and then popped to see her with tablets at nine o'clock. She didn't know what they were and didn't ask.

On day two, sweaty and tearful, she heard a commotion on the stairs. Raised voices, jarring, and heavy footfall. The bedroom door opened swiftly and banged against a bedside cabinet. The lamp wobbled.

"Daft git!" It was Dorothy. "Of course she will want to see her bloody mother!" She was calling over her shoulder. Betty rubbed her face roughly and attempted to straighten her hair. Dorothy marched over to Betty's side of the bed and frowned down at her.

William appeared in the doorway looking flustered and shrugged at Betty. '*Sorry*', he mouthed.

"Now then, my love. Oh, dear. Oh, dear. Let's get a clean nightie on you and I'll sit you up and brush your hair." She sat on the edge of the bed and pushed a loose strand away from Betty's face, and briefly stroked her cheek. "You make yourself useful for once and get some clean sheets and a wet flannel," she called over to William.

"Oh, Mum." Betty propped herself up, and buried herself into the soft warmth of her mother's belly.

Chapter Thirty-Six
Betty (Then)

Dorothy stayed several days, perhaps a week. William had been to visit her, trying to avoid any accusations of neglect on Betty's part, as she hadn't seen her mother in a little while. His visit hadn't gone as planned, it seemed. Rather than placating Dorothy, this news had opened up an unexpected desire to play nursemaid to her daughter and know every detail of her heath.

She had taken the bus and walked through the park to get to her, declaring she wasn't sure why she hadn't done it before. It was easy, really. She had turned up with an overnight bag, a bottle of tonic, and a steely determination to look after her only daughter.

She made chicken soup, and, in spite of the warm weather, Betty was glad of it and wolfed it down. She made sure Betty got out of bed at least once a day, to move about, wash, and allow Dorothy to strip the bed. Sometimes, Betty would wake to find her sitting on the other side of the bed, silently reading a newspaper or knitting. She didn't ask her any questions, and Betty was glad of it.

William reduced his visits to once a day. He was awkward and formal when he came in. He didn't touch her – she wasn't sure if he was scared of hurting her or if it was from embarrassment. She couldn't bear to see him; she wished he wouldn't come at all.

They still hadn't decorated the bedroom but she had always liked the space. The room was large and airy. It was at the rear of the house, and the window overlooked the back garden. There was no traffic there, and the long gardens on the terrace meant there was limited light. At night, it was quiet and still. In the morning, she awoke to birdsong. In spite of everything, she slept heavily, and often.

On the third or fourth day, Dorothy arrived with breakfast on a tray and a small envelope beside it.

"That tenant of yours came by. She left you this." She passed it over to Betty, who opened it, tearing the paper eagerly. The envelope had been reused; inside was another hummingbird sketch.

"Look!" she said, delighted, passing it to her mum.

"That is something," she said, holding it out at arm's length and peering over her glasses. From Dorothy, this was high praise.

"There's writing on the back," Betty said, having only noticed it when Dorothy held the small card aloft. She passed it back to her.

'*Let me know when you are well enough for visitors.*
Your friend for life x,' it said.

"I'd like to see her," Betty said.

"Humph." Dorothy rearranged Betty's pillow behind her so that she could sit comfortably to eat.

"What do you mean? Don't you think I should?" Betty asked. She was too tired to argue.

"Oh no, not me," Dorothy answered. "Your darling husband. He's been sending her away every day since I came here. We almost had a row over me bringing that blooming card up. '*She'll want her friend*,' I told him. She'll want to be around women."

"I can't believe it!" she said. "I had no idea. He knows how much we talk. She's been involved right from the start. I just can't believe it!"

"I can," Dorothy said. "I'm sorry, love, but I never have trusted that man of yours."

*

That evening, when William came to see her in the bedroom, she was ready. It was the first time that she had dressed since the day she came home. Somehow, the thought of being in nightwear made her feel he would have the upper hand. Her trousers were looser than they had been, she noted. Time to start rebuilding her health.

She tied her hair into a ponytail and waited for him, sat in the small yellow chair in the corner of the bedroom from half past four, anxiously picking at the skin on her thumb.

He didn't come home until 6pm. When he did, he came into the room carrying a large cardboard box. He was grinning broadly. This threw her, expecting his usual stiffness and formality.

"You're up!" he called, surprised. He placed the box on the foot of the bed.

"I need to start moving about and having visitors. Like Sandra," she said, pointedly. He didn't meet her eye and she was unsure if he had even noted what he said. There was a twitchy air about him. Excitement, almost.

"Good, yes. Getting up is a good idea. You can go downstairs tomorrow." He raised his eyebrows up and down. "You'll like that."

"Will I?"

"Oh, yes. You will *now*."

"William, what's going on?" She tapped her hand on the arm of the chair, quickly, eager to move him along.

"I got you this." He gestured to the box. "A present."

"Right. What is it?" She heard her voice – hollow and empty. She thought perhaps she should stand, move closer and show some gratitude or enthusiasm. But there was nothing there. She had nothing to draw on.

"I'll show you." The flaps of the box were loosely folded together. He lifted a large, cuboid item out. It was wrapped in bubble wrap. He placed it on the bed reverently, searching for the Scotch Tape that sealed it closed.

"Now, just wait a minute and I shall find it," he said, rubbing his fingernail along a seam.

"Can't you just tell me?"

"And spoil the surprise? You need to see this, darling." She heard herself sigh deeply; William either ignored it or failed to hear. "Aha!" he cried, finding the tape.

Carefully, he removed the packaging, lifting the parcel as he unrolled the wrapping over and under several times, in an irritating game of 'pass the parcel'. She vaguely wondered if it would be some sort of kitchen appliance. After several rounds of unpeeling, he turned to her and held out a hand.

"You must do the honours."

She got up, ignoring his proffered hand. She took a couple of steps to the bed. There were only one or two folds of bubble wrap left. Through the semi-opaque substance, she could see some sort of white leather box or case. She stayed still, looking until he guided her hands over. They removed the last of the packaging together.

It was a record player.

"There, I bet you never imagined you would have one of these? Top of the range, the young man in the shop tells me. I thought it would be better than your little transistor. I know you are partial to pop music."

"I… I don't know what to say." It seemed an odd gift for a husband to give his wife, under the circumstances.

"You could say that you love it? That you love me for getting it?" He moved closer to her, still smiling. He was so tickled by his ingenuity. "Don't you? Don't you, darling?" He put his hands on her shoulders and turned her to face him. She stayed back, at arms' length.

"It's very nice, yes. Thank you. I am sure I will use it at some point." Now she was the formal one.

"I thought it might help make you feel better," he said. "It might cheer you up."

"Cheer me up?" She turned away, the swift movement breaking his hold on her. She went back to the chair. "OK."

He sat down heavily on the bed. "Was it a bad idea? I thought it was a wonderful idea. I thought you'd simply love it." He rubbed his hands over his face, burying his fingertips in his eye sockets briefly, and then pinching the tip of his nose. "I don't know what to do," he said.

"You could start by letting me see my friends." Her voice was quiet. She did not want a row. She did not have the energy.

"What? Sandra, do you mean?"

"Who else?"

"Quite frankly, I thought she was the last person you'd want to see." He pulled his mouth into a tight pinch and winced. But he was wrong. The last person she wanted to see was him.

"Why? I can talk to her. And it saves me staring at the same walls all day."

"I can't bear it. I can't bear it when she comes around knocking on the door with her little tip-tappy noise and concerned eyes. Staring at me. Asking questions. I didn't want you to have that experience."

"But what's she ever done to you?"

"She was the one… she put the idea out there, didn't she. Of getting rid — "

"What? But that's not what happened. We didn't do it. We didn't go through with it." She paused. "We didn't need to."

"We would have, though. I think we would have. I would."

"I know you would. But how is that Sandra's fault?" She found herself gripping both arms of the chair to steady herself. There was a tremor within her, inside her bones.

"She made it possible, somehow. And I said it out loud. I wanted it. And now…" He trailed away, waving vaguely in her direction.

"Now what? This doesn't make any sense."

"I know. Give me a moment. I'm not entirely sure how to put this into words."

She recalled the last time he had said something akin to this. She needed him to try. She said nothing, waiting in the heavy silence, not prompting or comforting. It was his turn to be strong, now. His turn.

"I feel guilty," he said. "And angry. And confused. I wonder if we tempted fate, God, or whatever. I wonder if the universe or the baby knew how I felt. And that's why this has happened."

Betty frowned. "I've never known you to be superstitious... but I feel guilty, too. Not in that way. I feel guilty that my body let it down. That I wasn't strong enough, or there is something wrong with me, maybe. And that's why it didn't live. If anyone is responsible for... the loss... it has to be me. Me alone. So I feel it, the guilt, but for different reasons."

"I... but that's not what I mean. I don't feel guilty for tempting fate. I feel guilty because I'm glad that it's gone."

Chapter Thirty-Seven
Betty (Then)

The next day, Betty knocked on the door of Sandra's flat. Her mother was peeling potatoes for dinner and had announced she would be returning home that evening. She needed to check on her brother and that floozy of his – though she said so with a faint smile, Betty noted. Dorothy encouraged her to visit Sandra, apparently having forgotten about her qualms of mixing business and pleasure.

Sandra answered the door, her eyes opening wide at the sight of her. She went to throw her arms about her and then stopped herself.

"I am not that fragile," Betty said. "Honestly."

"It's more the staircase I was worried about!" she replied. She took her hand and led her down the stairs.

Sandra insisted that Betty sit in the chair, with her feet propped up, while she made her tea. A small jar of weeds sat on the side table beside her. Betty was glad to be there but had a strange, disconnected sensation as she listened to her talk. As if she was behind a pane of glass.

After a while, the tension started to drift away. She found herself becoming more animated as she told her about the horrors of the hospital, glad to find that in relaying it to Sandra the story could be consigned into the category of an amusing anecdote. She told her about matron, the liver, and the dreaded enema and its after-effects. Sandra howled with laughter, horrified.

"So you're glad to be home then. I've been asking your mum about you. She's been keeping me informed."

"Has she? How funny. I can't imagine the two of you together."

"We've been getting along rather well, actually. She's quite a force of nature, isn't she? One time I found myself sitting in front of oxtail soup before I knew it."

Betty smiled. "She is keen on feeding people up. Perhaps you have finally met your match in her. And she did say you'd been around. Thank you."

"And Mr William Williams? How is he? Is everything OK?

"I… no, not really. Things are difficult. But I suppose that's to be expected."

Sandra nodded. "Perhaps the two of you need a holiday together. You could go to Brighton or somewhere further afield. Spend some time, just the two of you, in the fresh air and with some lovely food."

"Now, that is an idea," Betty said, sitting back in the chair.

*

Betty made her way back upstairs after a couple of hours, to find her mother sitting on the sofa with her coat on, and William there, in his chair. He jumped up when he saw her. She noticed a glass of whisky on the side table by his seat and that familiar

212

look of agitation or excitement as he stalked towards her.

"What time is it?" Betty asked, wondering if she had been longer than she realised. "Have you been waiting for me?"

"Yes," he said. "Your mother is going home this evening. Soon. I thought you would want to say goodbye."

Dorothy sat, face impassive, handbag on her lap.

"Aren't you staying for tea, Mum?"

"Apparently not." She glanced over to William, pointedly.

"You are welcome, of course, Dorothy. I just thought you'd want to settle in before it got too late. Besides, I have something to talk to Betty about."

"So you said," Dorothy muttered.

"Darling, don't you think you are being a bit rude? Mum has been here for days. The least we can do is feed her." It was not like William to neglect his manners.

"Don't worry. I know when I have outstayed my welcome."

"Oh, Mum," she said, sitting down next to her. She glanced over at William, with a frown. "Perhaps a drink before you go?"

William jumped up again and walked towards the kitchen. "Brandy?" he asked.

"Brandy? At this time? Sherry, I should think," Dorothy said.

"I'll see what I can do."

Betty found herself leaning into her mum's shoulder, head dropped down. Dorothy made no comment but patted her hand, gently.

William appeared with two glasses of sherry. Betty was taken aback to be offered one, but said nothing and took it. Everyone sat in silence, clutching their small glasses until she got up and went over to the record player, for something to do. She only had two LPs, so selected Aretha Franklin over The Beatles, thinking this likely to cause the least comment from either of the others.

She noted that William started to tap his foot in time to the music. "What is this thing you want to tell me, then?" she asked.

He looked at Dorothy and shuffled in his seat. She had assumed it was something akin to the record player, or that they had been invited out, or something equally innocuous. Now she realised her mistake.

"Don't mind me. It won't be anything I haven't heard before."

But perhaps it would. Betty took a sip of her drink and grappled in her mind for a new topic of conversation.

"Actually, I had something to talk to you about, as well. I was just talking to Sandra and we... I wondered, perhaps we should have a little trip away? A holiday? It could be good for us."

"Wouldn't do any harm," her mum said.

"Per-haps," William said, tentatively. He was tapping his foot and looking around the room.

"Shall I do a bit of research? There's a travel agent on the edge of town, over near the school. Or if you wanted something simpler I could go to the train station and — "

"Actually, it's not good timing," he said, suddenly. "It might have to wait."

"I should think it's perfect timing," Dorothy snapped. "Maybe not for you, but for your wife. She's the one you should be thinking of."

"Why?" Betty asked.

"I've been given a promotion," he said, taking another gulp of whisky. "I'll be setting up a new office. Away. In Kent. I won't be… I will need to stay away. At least at the beginning."

Betty found herself leaning forward, mouth agape.

"It's good news, actually, darling. More money. Quite an honour," he said.

"It's good news," she repeated. "An honour."

"Yes, but then I guess more money means we can save up for an even better holiday, can't we? I shall be able to take you somewhere really fancy!" He was trying to make light but his words fell flat. His glass was empty now. His foot still drumming on the floor.

The music, his tapping, everything suddenly felt oppressive and loud. She couldn't think. She jumped up and went to the record player, snatching the arm abruptly so that the stylus scratched against the vinyl in a shriek.

She came back, sitting down heavily beside her mother. "But, now? Right now? Won't they let you wait a little?"

He didn't answer but shook his head.

"You bloody coward," Dorothy spat.

Chapter Thirty-Eight
Betty (Now)

The young people had stayed outside until late. When she left, Paul had his arm around April, who had snuggled into him and rested her head on his shoulder. Jonty was telling an outrageous anecdote that had them in stitches but didn't seem to have a climax. The sun had set and blankets and coats were draped over knees. Betty snuck away.

When she went to bed she could still hear them, but their faint voices and laughter were a comfort rather than an irritation as she lay there – a herbal tea and a small glass of whisky by her side. At one stage, there had even been a song.

Was she foolish to become so attached to her tenants? Sometimes she thought so. They were surrogate family, in a way, but better than no one. And it pleased her to watch them grow, and shift over time. It pleased her to help them where she could. Why not? She had very little family left to speak of: only Mark.

She had never imagined her life would be this way when she was their age. She remembered those early days of marriage and moving into the house. The expectations she had. The dreams.

She had been in Hummingbird House for almost fifty-five years, and many of those had been alone. Officially, she and William had been married for seventeen of those. That was what the records would show.

But the truth was far removed.

Mark, her nephew, had been one constant in her life – much more than her husband had been. John and Linda had moved into the top floor, less than a week before Linda gave birth to Mark. It had taken them much of that time to sort the belongings from the top floor. The majority of it was dumped in the end, having not been seen or used for over a year by then. Then they decorated and fit the place out. Betty and John had done this together. And it had helped to bring them closer, rather like the experience of dismantling and dumping the shed would have been for the others, tonight, she supposed.

There was a bathroom there, already, which had not been used since they had bought the house, blocked behind bags and boxes as it was. They made do with the fittings, and John had painted the walls a jolly lemon yellow colour that clashed with the sink but at least made the space look clean, and more cared for. Her mother had provided new towels and mats. Linda was delighted, she recalled. It was their first home. And they had stayed there for five years.

The kitchen was the biggest problem. There was nothing beyond the ground floor and the idea of sharing her space did not appeal greatly to Betty, but neither had it to Linda. Linda, it transpired, was not the most confident cook, and throwing two flights of stairs into the mix did not help. In the end, they had used money from William's promotion, combined with some of John's meagre savings (he did, in fact, have some) and created a small kitchenette in one of the bedrooms on the top floor: much more meagre and possibly less safe than what was there now – David had a fully fitted kitchen and dining area, with an integrated oven and a dishwasher. John and Linda had two hobs and a fridge. She didn't need an oven, apparently. Betty could still recall the face her mother had pulled at the thought of it.

In the first two years of Mark's life, they had settled into a routine: they shared a meal a couple of times each week, and she minded the baby whenever Linda went into the factory, which was four or five times a month. Linda had come to an arrangement with them to cover sickness and holidays for the other staff and seemed happy enough with this plan. As was Betty, who loved spending time with Mark. Sometimes Sandra joined them. Later, Linda returned to work full-time and Betty would often collect Mark from school.

She knew – everyone knew – that he was like a surrogate baby to her. The child she never had. But this was not a bad thing. The child had been showered in love. And she had been like a mother to him these last ten years, as both his parents had passed on.

In the months after she lost the baby, William's promotion took him away often. She didn't know if this was avoidable or by choice, and was nervous to ask. Initially, it had been a week, then two weeks at a time. Eventually, he was away for up to four weeks and returned for a flying visit in between. Of course, they had the telephone by then, so they did speak, though not every day.

He hardly got to know Mark at all.

After the first ten months or so of travelling, he had come home one day with the suggestion that he rent a flat. He was tired of living out of a suitcase, in faceless hotels.

She had been shocked. It had not occurred to her that they were living apart – but of course, in essence, they were. They could go three or four days or more without speaking. Three or four weeks without seeing each other. Something had been broken by all that had befallen them. Something fragile that they could never repair. She no longer felt the flicker in her stomach when she was near him. And she no longer had that absolute trust.

This was the separation that Sandra had proposed a year earlier. The one they could not even countenance.

He could get some financial help from work, towards the cost of the rent. So it was a logical step.

She had agreed.

That Sunday night he had travelled back on the train, and she knew things would never be the same. The end had started without her even realising it, and the thing that had upset her the most – the thing that made her cry – was that by then neither of them truly minded. Perhaps he was not who she had thought he was at all. Never had been.

His next visit to Hummingbird House was three weeks later. They had both made an effort to pretend that there was nothing significant in this step – see, I still visit. See, we are still a couple. This is just a practical decision. Nothing momentous. But the charade didn't last. Three weeks became four again. Then six. Then months. By that stage, they

219

both called it a 'visit', not a trip home. His home was away, further north, in his one-bedroom flat and with the colleagues and friends she had never met.

In the last two and a half years of his life, he didn't visit her at all.

*

The next morning, she awoke early as usual, but she felt surprisingly refreshed. Her legs ached from all the standing and walking the day before, though her head was clear and her spirits lifted. She read a couple of chapters of her book before rising, stretching out and enjoying the luxury. Eventually, the bathroom called her and she decided to get up.

She still had some cleaning up to do: the glasses had been left outside her backdoor, as was customary, and she had the bin to empty, and dishes on the rack to put away. She had turned on her radio and found herself humming along to The Mamas & the Papas, her thoughts drifting in and out of memories, today, and yesterday.

Content with her work, she then sat at her table, treating herself to loose-leaf tea and scrambled eggs for breakfast. She was surprised to find it was already almost ten by the time she finished.

Before she had left the party the night before, she had promised Jonty that she would come upstairs for morning coffee. She wondered how he would be feeling today and whether he would have any regrets for overindulging or staying up late the night before his mother arrived.

She picked up her radio and carried it into the bedroom to enjoy the music while she dressed. She wanted to wear something cheerful today. Something striking. She flicked through her wardrobe, dismayed at how many brown trousers and dark tops greeted her. This would never do. Perhaps a shopping trip was in order. Perhaps she should take her own advice, and visit the hairdresser, too. Maybe she would even go with April.

Eventually, she settled on peacock shades of greens and blues.

*

A little before 11 am, she knocked on Jonty and Ben's door. Ben opened, again in jogging bottoms and a vest top.

"Come in, come in," he said, leaning in to kiss her cheek. "Fabulous 'do', as usual, Betty. Now, he's off in the bedroom with Mum but I really must go and shower. I've been sweating like a sow and I can smell myself from here."

He closed the door behind her and gestured to the double doors that led to the bedroom at the front of the house.

"Go ahead," he said. "He'll probably be glad of the interruption." He winked at her, then walked away.

Betty hesitated, as she wondered if it was appropriate to go to his bedroom like this but then decided to follow his lead. As she made her way to the bedroom she could hear animated voices through the crack in the double doors.

It was a woman's voice. "I cannot believe you have still got that ghastly painting. And above your bed, of all places!"

"Hush. I love that painting and you know it. It'll be worth a fortune one day," Jonty replied.

"Only if it becomes fashionable to buy paintings with questionable perspectives."

Betty stood for a moment, holding the handle of the door, watching the two of them, their intimacy and comfort. They stood at the bottom of the bed, gazing up at the picture. Their body language mirrored one another. Their jaw, mouth, nose alike.

Oxo the cat took this opportunity to try to squeeze out, clearly keen to have respite from the situation. There was an unexpected noise as he creaked the door further open and she moved to the side to let him by. They looked over at her, in unison.

"Hello, Sandra," said Betty, and smiled.

*

Searching for Sandra – a novella.

Book Three in the Hummingbird House Series.
Out now.

About the Author

Jane Harvey is a pen name. 'Jane' crafts fun fiction for the thinking woman, where she enjoys exploring unexpected friendships and writing happy endings. This is lucky because, in real life, her (prize-winning) fiction is a little bleaker. She was born and raised on the island of Jersey, where she also works for a mental health charity.

Acknowledgements

Thank you to my beta readers: Lily, Mary, Cheryl, and Averil, and my proofreader, Sara-Jane.

A special thank you to all the readers of Book One who encouraged me to keep telling the stories from Hummingbird House. There are many more to come.

ALSO BY

Dreena Collins

*Jane Harvey is the pen name of Dreena Collins.
Dreena writes literary short stories*

Embers (Tales of Courage and Comeuppance)

She Had Met Liars Before: Six Very Short Stories of Strength and Survival

Taste: Six of the Best (Six Readers' Favourites from previous works)

Collected (The Complete Stories: The Blue Hour Series plus Bird Wing)

Bird Wing (A Flash Fiction Collection)

The Day I Nearly Drowned (Short Stories Vol. Two)

The Blue Hour (Short Stories Vol. One)

Unsure about short stories? Turn over for an excerpt from Embers…

One
Embers

We are three shades of red. Auburn, copper, sand. Dutifully, we tilt our heads together for the photograph – my sisters leaning in, their long hair falling around my shoulders until we become one tangled mass. Mum is delighted at the sight of their thick manes, disguising my short crop. Susie rests a strand of hair over my head, her cheek pressing hard against mine.

Her hair is closest in colour to dad's. She is a reprint of him, but softer. An echo. It's their turn now, and she laughs when dad suggests she sit on his knee. Eventually, they stand back-to-back, arms folded, propping one another up. Their hair is burnished, metallic. Elizabethan fire.

He kisses her forehead after Mum takes the picture and then runs back to the barbeque, turning the last few pieces of meat over the dying heat.

Then Susie and Jennifer are together. Jennifer suggests they sit on the rug. Somehow, they know how to pose, how to languish and lounge and laugh in a freeze-frame…

226

Printed in Great Britain
by Amazon